The Second Shooter

E. A. Briginshaw

E. A. Briginshaw
MARCH 4/2015

ISBN: 978-0-9921390-4-9 (Book)
ISBN: 978-0-9921390-5-6 (eBook)

ACKNOWLEDGMENTS

Although the novel is a work of fiction, some of the characters are composite characters based on my family and friends. Thanks to all of the people who reviewed and critiqued numerous drafts of this novel including friends, members of my family and writers from the London Writers Society. Special thanks to Gary Barwin, Writer-in-Residence at the University of Western Ontario and the London Public Library for his help with several key chapters.

E. A. BRIGINSHAW

*** CHAPTER 1 ***

Stan gave a heavy sigh as he saw his boss approaching him with a worried look on his face. Stan was sure that he had already come to check up on him at least twenty times today.

"How are things coming along?" his boss asked, giving a false smile that failed to hide his concern.

"About the same as the last time you asked," Stan replied with a scowl. Stan was the team supervisor with the National Archives who had been assigned to deal with a recent influx of documents and files related to the assassination of President John F. Kennedy. According to the JFK Records Act of 1992, all records related to the assassination had to be released within 25 years of the enactment of that legislation. This was crunch time, as the deadline of October 26, 2017 was quickly approaching.

"Let me know if you run into any problems," his boss said as he headed back to his office.

Stan knew he would be back again shortly. "It would be great if you could give me about ten more people to help," Stan muttered to himself, "or God forbid, sit down at a keyboard yourself". But Stan knew neither was going to happen. The Assassination Records Review Board had not been given enough staff or time to properly complete its mandate and many people had quit in frustration over the years.

Stan glanced at his cell phone to make sure he hadn't missed a text from his wife. He would have quit working here himself, except his wife was due with their second child at any moment. They couldn't afford to be without health benefits at this point in their lives.

Stan clicked his mouse to open another folder of files on his computer. The files consisted of digitized images of the thousands of police reports, photos and videos that had been filed regarding the assassination. The only records not required to be released were those designated by the President where their release would cause an identifiable harm to the military defense, intelligence operations, law enforcement, or conduct of foreign relations. Furthermore, the identifiable harm must be of such gravity that it outweighed the public interest in disclosure.

The President, to his credit, had recently turned down requests from the Secret Service, the FBI and the CIA to prevent the release of thousands of documents. There were some who thought that one or more of those organizations had somehow been involved in the assassination, but others felt they didn't want the documents released because it showed how incompetent they had been that day in protecting the President. The declassification of many of those documents had dramatically increased the amount of work required over the last few weeks.

Stan saw his boss heading toward him once again. "I'm not going to get this done if you keep interrupting me."

His boss took another look at his watch and headed back to his office. Stan could see that it was now 5:30 p.m. and the office was practically empty. Most of the other employees had already headed home, knowing that the latest salary freeze prevented them from getting paid for any overtime. Stan, as a supervisor, didn't qualify and his boss had reminded him numerous times that he was expected to work whatever hours were required to get the job done.

For the next few hours, Stan continued to review the files that had been prepared by his staff and then upload them to the National Archives website. He flew through the folders that had been prepared by most of his staff, as he trusted their work. However, the files prepared by Jamie would require closer scrutiny as he was a junior clerk and was known to be somewhat sloppy in his work. It took Stan about an hour to go through his files and it appeared that he had done a good job. However, he knew he had several more hours of work ahead when he opened the last folder. It didn't appear to have any organization at all and everything in the directory was simply labelled with sequential numbers.

Suddenly his cell phone chirped and the display showed the call was from his wife. "It's time," she said. "My water just broke. Mom is taking me to the hospital. Can you meet us there?"

"I'll be there as soon as I can. Twenty minutes max."

After he hung up the phone, he could see there were at least a few hundred files he had left to review. But the birth of his child took precedence over the release of documents about the death of a President that had happened over fifty years earlier. Who would care at this point?

He saw his boss emerge from his office and start walking toward him. He quickly selected the remaining files and clicked on the button to upload them to the National Archives website.

"All done," Stan said as he grabbed his coat and started

toward the door.

He did not realize the sequence of events he had just started with a simple click of his mouse.

*** CHAPTER 2 ***

Henry Shaw watched as his two sons carried the last few boxes from the house out to the small truck he had rented for the move. Henry had already taken several loads and he could feel the twinge in his back telling him it was time to let his sons handle the rest. He was approaching his mid-forties and he was finding that he couldn't do what the young guys do anymore, something that annoyed him immensely.

David, Henry's youngest son, was heading off to Wilfrid Laurier University in Waterloo, Ontario. David had just turned nineteen and was the athlete of the family. He was tall and thin and it was impossible to miss the resemblance from his father's side of the family.

"I think that's everything," David said.

"Let me give it one last check," Henry said as he headed back into the house. As Henry surveyed his son's empty room, he felt overwhelmed. Both of his sons would soon be out on their own.

Robert, his oldest son, was twenty-two and just starting his second year in mathematics at Waterloo. Robert had graduated high school a few years ago, but it had taken him a while to figure out what he wanted to do with his life. Henry was pleased when he announced that he was going to the University of Waterloo, Henry's alma mater.

Henry looked out the bedroom window and saw both boys sitting on the back of the truck. While David looked like his father's side of the family, Robert looked like his mother's. Henry wished his wife could see how both of their boys had grown up, but she had died of cancer a few years ago. He fought back the tears that he could feel welling up and started scanning the room for anything they might have forgotten. He saw the soccer jerseys still pinned to the wall. One was David's jersey from the Under-19 Canadian national team. Beside it were jerseys from the American and British teams they had played against in a tournament.

"Aren't you going to take your jerseys with you?" Henry asked David when he got outside.

"No, it's probably best to leave them here. I'm hoping to put some new ones up at our place in Waterloo."

David was a sure-bet to make the soccer team at Laurier and was hoping to make the Canadian national team, but that was less certain. He would now be competing against full-grown men, not aspiring teenagers like he had with the U19 squad.

They were heading to Waterloo a few weeks earlier than the regular students, as tryouts for school teams began before the semester started. Henry was pleased that both of his sons would be rooming together at a new residence, built in partnership between the University of Waterloo and Wilfrid Laurier University. In fact, both of them rooming together was a forgone conclusion as David had started a new business venture called SchoolRoommate.com which proposed to provide better roommate matching at residences. David had tested the software matching program using himself and his brother as guinea pigs. He hadn't been successful in selling the software to either university, but they had agreed to try it out for their new joint-partnership residence.

"Okay, let's go," Henry said as they climbed into the moving truck.

Robert and David played rock-paper-scissors to see who had to sit in the middle on the bench seat in the truck; David lost. But that didn't dampen his spirit at all.

"The three amigos begin their venture to take over the world!" David announced as Henry put the truck into gear.

* * *

As they approached the new residence, Henry was directed onto a makeshift path as the main entrance was blocked by a paver laying asphalt on the roadway and parking lot. They were told to park about a hundred metres from the main entrance.

"Are you sure this place is ready for you to move in?" Henry asked.

There were numerous tradesmen wearing hardhats still working on various aspects of the building. "Hold up there!" one of the workers yelled to them as soon as they started to walk toward the building. A truck filled with construction materials emitted a deafening *beep-beep* sound as it backed up in front of them.

"It's supposed to be completely done by the time the regular students arrive in a few weeks", David shouted over the din, "but they promised our section would be ready by now."

"Don't worry Dad," Robert said. "I'm sure we'll be fine."

When they finally made their way to the main lobby, they

had to walk between two rows of pylons as a tradesman was putting grout on the new tile floors and another was installing light fixtures. They headed into the elevator, which had tarps on the walls to prevent any damage during the construction and move-in period. They were pleased when the elevator doors opened to reveal the construction was completed on the third floor.

"We're supposed to be in W308," David said as he pointed down the west hallway. When they got there, the door was open and it looked ready for them to move in. W308 consisted of two small bedrooms, each with built-in desks and shelving. They were separated by a small common area containing two lounge chairs that looked like they came from a military surplus store, a coffee table, a fridge and a sink. The bathrooms and showers were down the hall, shared among the occupants of the eight rooms in their pod.

The rooms were sparsely furnished. Each tenant was expected to provide some of their own belongings to make it feel more like home. Henry had agreed to let the boys bring an old loveseat from his basement and some other things he really didn't use any more. The boys had also talked him into letting them "*borrow*" a big-screen TV, but Henry knew he'd never get it back.

Suddenly a blast from the fire alarm outside their room pierced the air.

"Don't worry," one of the tradesmen yelled to them when they came out into the hallway. "You can ignore the alarm. We'll be testing it for another few hours." Sure enough, the alarm stopped about thirty seconds later.

They spent the next hour or so lugging their belongings from the small moving truck up to their room. It would have taken less time except they continually had to maneuver around the tradesmen in the lobby. They also had to wait for the elevator when one of the workers commandeered it to move supplies up to another floor.

"Do you want me to help you get things unpacked and organized?" Henry asked his sons.

"No, I think we've got it from here," David said. He took a box from his father and put it in the corner of the room with all of the others.

Both boys immediately started setting up their computers in their respective rooms. They both had the latest-and-greatest computers, claiming they needed the power for their schoolwork, but Henry knew that the high-speed processors and graphics cards were mostly for their games.

Henry felt totally useless at this stage and didn't know what else he should be doing to help. It was Robert who noticed. "It looks like someone needs a hug."

He was right. Henry did need a hug. He wasn't ready for his sons to be out on their own.

"Don't worry, we'll be fine," Robert said. "We'll get all of this mess organized eventually. Is Laura coming up this weekend?"

Laura Walsh was the woman who had come into Henry's life a few years after their mother had died. She lived in Chicago and Henry lived in the suburbs of Toronto, so they didn't see each other as often as Henry would like. However, the law firm that Henry worked for had merged with a Chicago firm so Henry used that as an excuse for as many trips to Chicago as he could. Henry wasn't a lawyer; he was the Information Technology Manager for the firm.

"No, she said she couldn't get away this weekend. She's working on some big story." Laura was an investigative journalist with the Chicago Tribune. Lately, it seemed like she was always working on a big story.

"Well, if you guys don't need anything else, I should

probably get the rental truck back." Henry was hoping for an objection, but none came. Both boys gave him one last hug and he headed back out to the truck.

It was just over an hour's drive from Waterloo to the suburb outside of Toronto where Henry lived. He wasn't looking forward to returning to an empty house. His mother had lived with them for a few years, except for the winter months which she spent in Florida, but even she had recently moved to live with Henry's sister. With the boys all grown up now, she didn't think they needed her help anymore.

As he drove, Henry thought about Laura and how they had first met in the airport bar in Chicago – a night he would never forget. When he got home, the house seemed bigger and lonelier than ever, so he decided he would head to Chicago in the morning to see her. He was sure she would love the surprise. He was wrong.

*** CHAPTER 3 ***

David turned on his computer and was surprised that he didn't see a private secured network for their building. "You seeing a network connection for our residence?" he yelled to Robert.

"No," Robert yelled back. "Maybe it's not set up yet."

"Well they can't expect us to stay here without Internet access. I've got the number of the building manager. We were told to call him if we have any problems."

David called the building manager using his cell phone, but it went straight to voice-mail. The message said the manager could be found in the administration office, so they both headed off to find him. When they arrived, they found him sitting in his office surrounded by a wall of unopened boxes. He was a middle-aged man who loved kids and wanted to be a teacher, but a recent downsizing had forced him to consider other options. He much preferred dealing with eight-year-olds who thought he was smart and looked up to him, rather than the university-aged kids who thought they already knew everything.

"We don't have Internet access," David said as they

navigated around the boxes.

The building manager sighed. The last thing he needed was another problem to deal with. "Yeah, it's not set up yet."

He was hoping they would simply leave. They didn't.

"What's your name and what room are you in?" he finally asked.

"I'm David Shaw and this is my brother Robert. We're in W308."

"David Shaw," the manager said. "You're the kid who designed the roommate matching program, aren't you? That's another problem I'm dealing with. I can't figure out how it works." He pointed to his computer which was displaying an error.

Robert sensed they weren't going to get a quick resolution to any of their problems and tried a different approach. He knew it was important to get off on the right foot with the building manager. "I'm sure David can help you with that and maybe I can help you with the network problem."

"Do you know anything about phones, networks and computers?"

"Yep, I'm in computer science at UW," Robert said, "so I know enough to get me in trouble."

"Well, let's tackle the network problem first," the building manager said to both of them. "Grab a box and I'll show you what to do." Robert and David each grabbed a box from the pile in the office. "I'm Scott Porter by the way," the building manager continued. "Sorry to be so short with you, but all of this was supposed to be completed by now, so I'm a bit under the gun."

"No problem," Robert said. "I can't imagine trying to get all of this organized before all of the students arrive."

"The computer network is actually tied into our phone

system," Scott said as he showed them how his phone and computer were connected. "Paul, the telecom guy, said it's faster and more secure than having a wireless network. So, if your phone isn't working, that means he hasn't finished wiring them up yet and your computer connection won't work either. He's working in the wiring closet down at the end of the hall. He might be able to make yours a priority if you ask him nicely."

Robert and David headed down the hall in search of the wiring closet. "Hello," Robert said as he peered into the tiny room.

"Hi guys," Paul said as he peeked out from behind the matrix of equipment and wires. "What can I do for you?"

"We just moved into W308 and wondered how long it would be until we get our network connection," Robert said.

"Well I'm doing them in batches of sixteen and I'm still working on the first floor, so it could be a while." He could tell from the silent response that wasn't the answer they were hoping for. "But I'll make you a deal. If you take phones up for 301 to 308 and plug them in, I'll hook yours up next."

"Deal," Robert and David said in unison.

* * *

"The network speed is amazing!" David yelled to his brother. They were part of a team playing an online game called *League of Legends* and they were easily overpowering their opponents. They continued to play for several more hours until Robert finally said he had to get some sleep as they were now into the wee-hours of the morning.

"Good night," David said as he shut the door to his bedroom. He knew he should probably get some sleep as well, but he had one more thing he wanted to do that night.

He pulled his soccer bag out of the pile of boxes and carefully pulled a black laptop computer from the bottom of it. This laptop looked like a homemade device as it didn't have any logos or labels identifying the manufacturer. He unplugged his school computer from the network and plugged in the laptop.

"Please enter your password." prompted the screen as soon as he turned the laptop on.

David carefully entered the twenty-four character combination of upper and lower-case letters and numbers of the password. He had finally memorized the limerick his uncle Alan had taught him so he no longer had to have it written down. He remembered the day they had run laps together around the track at his high school when he had promised his uncle he would carry on with his work if anything should happen to him. At the time, he was sure that it was just something from his uncle's bipolar fantasy world, but it had turned out to be so much more.

"Welcome, Goliath" appeared on the screen.

Goliath was his uncle's code-name in their secret society and it was now David's code-name. His uncle had died in a mysterious plane crash along with Edward Bronson, the media magnate who had founded the group. The police suspected the plane had been tampered with, but they had never proven anything. Over a year had passed since the plane had been found, so it was doubtful anything further would come of it.

The secret society was now headed by Simon Westbrook. David didn't know much about him as he had only met him once, at his uncle's funeral. Simon had told him he was Edward Bronson's lawyer and that he would be continuing on his client's legacy and heading up the group. In reality, the fact that the society existed was no longer that much of a secret. However, no one seemed to know the identities of those in the organization, or how large it was.

David had been intrigued by the organization and its goals from the first day his uncle had told him about it. It frustrated him that politicians spent more time trying to destroy each other and gain power than they did trying to solve the major issues facing the world. That's why there weren't any politicians allowed in the group. The world is full of really smart people – they just had to create a way for all of them to work together. David had always been driven to find a new way to solve things when the old ways failed to work anymore.

"*Retrieve instructions*," David typed into the computer.

For months, David had not received any communications and he had stopped checking for messages on a daily basis. Now, he only checked about once a week, if that. He was surprised to see a new message on his computer.

"*Please distribute files to all associates for analysis*," the message on the screen said. There appeared to be several hundred files in the list. David had no idea what was in the files, nor was he supposed to know. He was simply the middle-man, the courier responsible for delivering messages to his contacts, six people in total.

David clicked on a tiny icon that appeared in the lower right portion of his screen. A small door opened on the side of the laptop and a tray slid out. But this was not to load a CD – it was much too small for that. David pulled a small microchip from his soccer bag, placed it onto the tray and pushed it back into the computer.

"*Package created*," appeared on the screen when the copy of the first set of files completed. Because there were so many files, he had to use seven separate microchips to complete the process.

David knew that he would have to distribute each of the

microchips to his contacts. Originally, the chips had been sewn into hems or pockets of clothes, as they were small enough to be easily hidden, but they had expanded the methods of distribution since then. They could also be easily inserted into cell phones, children's toys or MP3 players without detection. David knew the methods he would use to distribute the microchips to his six contacts. But he had a problem; he had seven microchips and only six contacts.

"*Packages created and ready for distribution to contacts,*" he typed into the computer. "*Require additional contact to complete distribution.*"

David could see the sun starting to come up and he hadn't had any sleep yet. He knew he had to be up in a few hours to head to the first soccer tryout, so he threw himself onto his bed and was asleep within seconds.

* * *

Robert was awakened by someone knocking on the door of their suite, but it took him a few seconds to recognize his new surroundings. The knock repeated, this time a little louder. When he opened the door, he saw Paul, the telecom guy, standing there holding a bunch of boxes.

"Good morning," Paul said. "I was wondering whether you and your brother wanted to make a few quick bucks helping me set up the rest of the phones in the building. I'm way behind and I could sure use some help."

Robert was always looking for a way to pick up a few extra dollars. "Sure, I can help, but I think my brother has already headed off for soccer tryouts." He could see the note from David taped to the back of the door saying he wouldn't be back until after 2:00 p.m.

"Well, beggars can't be choosers. I'll be working down in the wiring closet and I'll tell you what I need done using this," Paul said as he handed Robert a two-way radio. "But basically, I need you to grab phones from the manager's office and install them in each room on the second, third and fourth floors and then verify that they're working. It will save me from running back and forth from the wiring closet."

"Sounds pretty simple," Robert said.

They spent the next few hours installing the phones and most worked without any problems. However, they started encountering problems after the first sixty-four had been installed. Robert knew the problem was serious when he saw Paul looking in the manual. He knew referring to the documentation was usually the last resort for techies.

"Okay, I think I've figured it out," Paul said. "I have to bridge the two network cabinets, but that means I'm going to have to push out a software update to each of the phones we've already installed."

"Will that take long?" Robert asked.

"Not long at all, but I'd suggest you disconnect your computers from the network while I do it. It shouldn't cause any problems, but I'd hate to corrupt anything on your computer by accident."

Robert headed back to his room to disconnect his computer from the network. He was going to do the same for David's computer, but was surprised to find that David had locked his room before heading out.

"My computer is unplugged, but my brother's is still connected and his room is locked," Robert said into the two-way radio.

"Ooh, that makes me nervous," Paul replied. "Can you back-up your brother's files before I push out the update?"

Robert plugged his computer back in and was pleased to see that he could access David's computer over the network. As a techie, Robert knew how important it was to make regular backups. He also knew it had been over a month since he had backed up his own data, so this was a timely reminder. He plugged a portable drive into the USB port of his computer and started copying everything from both his and David's computer onto the portable drive.

"It says it should take almost an hour to do the backup," Robert said into the walkie-talkie.

"No problem," Paul said. "It's time for lunch anyway. Care to join me?"

Paul showed up at Robert's room a few minutes later with a huge lunch-kit. "My wife always makes enough to feed an army when I head off to do one of these installs. I keep trying to tell her I can just grab something close by, but she won't hear of it. Help yourself – there's more than enough."

They talked as they ate and Paul found that Robert reminded him of his own son – smart, full of dreams. If all kids were like them, the future was in good hands.

Robert watched as the data was copied onto the portable drive and was surprised at how much there was. After it was completed, he unplugged the portable drive and put it into his backpack. He made a mental note to store the backup in his locker the next time he went to the university.

* * *

David arrived back from soccer tryouts a few hours later. Things hadn't gone well. His lack of sleep the night before meant he hadn't been particularly sharp. As he unlocked his door, he was alarmed to see that he had neglected to put away his laptop before leaving that morning, more evidence that he wasn't firing on all cylinders. He wiggled the mouse which caused the screen to come to life and saw that he had a new message.

"*Distribute the packages to your six contacts,*" the message on the screen said. *"Someone will contact you to get the seventh."*

He shut down the laptop and hid it back inside the secret compartment of his soccer bag. He wondered who would be contacting him.

*** CHAPTER 4 ***

Laura's condo was on the north side of Chicago and initially it had taken Henry quite a while to figure out the colour-coded system used by the Chicago transit system. But now that he was more familiar with it, he found it a much easier way to get around the city. He glanced at the transit map above the door and could see that the Clark/Division stop was next.

It was a beautiful day in Chicago and it wouldn't take him long to walk the rest of the way to Laura's condo. He had taken the first flight out from Toronto that morning and with the one-hour time difference between the cities, he was confident he would surprise Laura before she headed into work.

But as he approached Laura's building, he was the one taken by surprise. Todd, Laura's old boyfriend, emerged from the building and got into his car in one of the visitor's parking spots. Henry had met Todd before. Laura had told him all about Todd and how they had lived together for almost six years, but that now they were just friends who were focused on their respective careers. Todd worked for the FBI and looked like he should be the poster-boy to recruit people to join their force. He was about eight years younger than Henry, about the same age as Laura, and obviously in very good shape. Henry suddenly felt very old as he slowly continued his walk toward Laura's building. When he got to the entrance, he just stood there wondering if he should buzz her unit or simply turn around and head back home. His decision was made for him when one of the tenants entering the building held the door open for him.

"Thanks," Henry said.

"I haven't seen you for a while," the tenant said. He had recognized Henry from one of his previous visits to see Laura. "Been doing some travelling?"

"I've been in Toronto for a few weeks. This is actually my girlfriend's place."

"Nice," the tenant said, whatever that meant. "Have a good day," he said as he got off the elevator.

Henry rode up to the tenth floor, but paused before entering Laura's condo. She had given him a key to her place several months ago but he always felt a little weird about using it. He paused outside her door, but finally decided to give it three soft knocks.

"Go away. I'm busy and I'm not buying anything," Laura yelled from inside.

It wasn't quite the warm greeting Henry was hoping for. "It's Henry," he said through the door.

"What are you doing here?" she said as she threw open the door. Before Henry could answer, she held up her hand. "Sorry, but I'm on a call," she whispered to him.

"Yeah, well tell him I need him to keep digging," she said to whoever was on the phone. "They're not going to just hand us this stuff on a platter." Laura walked back to her desk which was covered with papers and rifled through them until she found what she was looking for.

Even though she was dressed in just a T-shirt and sweatpants, Henry was once again overwhelmed by her beauty. Laura was a tall, thin brunette who seemed to move with the grace of a dancer. She had the smoothest, softest skin he had ever touched, but it was her blue eyes that Henry loved to watch. They seemed to dance as she thought about what she was going to say next. Laura was an investigative journalist with the Chicago Tribune and she was very good at her job. Her eyes could almost hypnotize a person into revealing everything they knew. Henry had always thought she was way out of his league. Maybe she was.

"Okay, I should be in the office within the hour," Laura said as she hung up the phone.

She turned her attention to Henry. "Sorry, but you caught me at a bad time. I'm trying to make some progress on a story, but I'm just treading water at best. I promised my editor I'd have something for him today, so I'm not sure how much time I'll have for you."

She could see the disappointed look on Henry's face. "I was just about to step into the shower. Care to join me?"

"No, it sounds like you've got a busy day ahead of you."

His response caught Laura by surprise and she immediately sensed something else was bothering him. "I'll just be a minute and then we can talk." She started removing her T-shirt and sweatpants as she walked down the hall toward the bathroom. "You know where I am if you change your mind."

Henry turned away and headed out onto the balcony. Even though her building was several blocks away, she had a beautiful view of Lake Michigan which was perfectly calm this morning. It was only a few minutes later when Laura joined him on the balcony. Her short, dark hair was still wet, but she flipped it into place with her fingers. Even though she wasn't wearing any makeup, she still looked like a million bucks.

"So this was a nice surprise. What prompted you to come to Chicago?"

"You said you're working on a big story and couldn't get up to Toronto, so I thought I'd come here instead."

"You're such a sweetie." She gave him a hug. "Feeling a bit lonely?"

"Yeah, the boys moved into their residence at university and the house seems so empty right now."

"I'm really busy, but I'm sure I can fit a little time in for you."

"So, what's the big story you're working on?"

"The government accidently released a bunch of documents last week and now they're trying to get them all back. They're threatening anyone who downloaded them and makes them public with charges of treason or terrorism. They're using the *Patriot Act* once again to bully people into submission."

They both headed back inside the condo when the coffee maker signaled that the coffee was ready. Laura poured Henry the first cup while she pulled a clean mug from the dishwasher.

"What's in the documents?" Henry asked as he sat on the white leather couch and took his first sip of coffee.

"Nobody knows, and that's what I'm trying to find out. I've already followed up with some of my usual contacts at places like *Wikileaks*, but they say they don't know anything."

"Don't they always say that?"

"Yeah, but this time I think they're just as confused as I am. If they've got something, they don't know what it is yet either."

"It's usually something like the U.S. bombing some place they weren't supposed to, or caught spying on some other country," Henry said. "What's so special about this one?"

"No one knows. Nobody's talking. I've already called all of my insiders and got nothing."

Henry paused and took an extra sip of coffee before asking his next question. "Speaking of insiders, do you ever contact your old boyfriend at the FBI? What was his name again, Todd?"

Laura let out a heavy sigh. "Ah, there it is," she said as she put down her coffee mug. "I knew there was something bothering you."

She came over and took Henry's coffee and placed it on the coffee table. Then she straddled him on the couch so she could look directly into his eyes. "You know his name and you saw him here earlier this morning, didn't you?"

"Maybe," Henry said, trying to avoid eye contact.

She grabbed his face and forced him to look at her. "We're friends - that's all. I asked him to pop over to see if he knew anything about the leaked documents, which he didn't. Now, don't you feel stupid for thinking what you've been thinking?"

"Yeah, I'm sorry," Henry said. He felt relieved to hear her explanation. "I'll make it up to you."

"You're damn right you will," Laura said as she started taking off her clothes.

"I thought you said you had to get into the office."

"I do, but this won't take long," she said as she pushed Henry down on the couch. She was right. She got what she needed and was still in the office within the hour.

*** CHAPTER 5 ***

The building manager stared at the error message on his computer screen. He had no idea what "*database connection error*" meant or what to do about it.

"Good morning, Mr. Porter," David said when he walked into the office a few minutes later.

"Just call me Scott. I hope you know how to fix this because I need the rooms allocated by next week."

David had designed the roommate matching program, but he wasn't really a techie. Although he had figured out the questions to ask the applicants and fine-tuned the algorithm to find the best matches for roommates, he had contracted someone else to do the programming.

"Let's try re-booting the server," David said.

"Yeah, I thought about giving it a good swift kick with my boot," Scott said under his breath.

David laughed. "If it doesn't work, I've got someone that I can call."

They watched as the computer started up again. When it did, David logged in to the application. This time, no error message appeared. "It was probably just caused by all of the changes in the network configuration." David navigated to the screen that showed the assigned roommates.

"Could you print that out for me?" Scott asked. "I'm more of a pen-and-paper kind of guy."

"Sure," David said. He clicked on the printer icon and the report started coming out of the printer on the credenza beside Scott's desk.

Scott scanned the report. "Some of these students won't be coming here after all – said they decided to go somewhere else. How do I delete them from our system and assign their room to someone else?"

David showed him how to delete those students from the system. "Now we just run the matching program again. It'll fill the vacancies using the most suitable roommates from those on the waiting list."

The program filled in a few of the vacancies with names, but there were still a few that had "TBD" listed.

"So what am I supposed to do with a TBD?" Scott asked.

"That means *To Be Determined*. It means they haven't completed the comprehensive questionnaire yet. You should contact them to have them complete the survey and then the system will match them up with the best fit."

"Are you sure this is all worth it?" Scott knew that this meant he had a few more things added to his to-do list.

"Yeah, it's pretty important. An incompatible roommate can mess up a student's whole year. Some of our surveys have indicated it has caused some students to fail a term or drop out of school altogether." David remembered using those exact same words when he had pitched his system to the universities. "Let me know when you get those surveys back and I'll come and help you match them up."

David glanced at his watch. "I've got to head off to

soccer practice right now, but feel free to call me if you have any problems."

"You can count on it," Scott said.

* * *

Alex sailed a corner-kick into the box and David easily headed it into the empty net. Alex was normally a defender and was rarely given the opportunity to take corner kicks, but they were just playing around before the practice began on Alumni Field. Alex Bujaczek had been David's best friend all through high school and it was no coincidence they had chosen to go to the same university. They had intentionally applied to the same universities.

Both of them had played for the Under-19 Canadian national soccer team and they were sure bets to make the university squad. However, they were also hoping to make the Canadian national team, which was less of a certainty. They knew the scouts would be watching players from all of the universities to select the most promising prospects.

"David," the coach yelled from the sideline. "Alex," he yelled again. "I need to speak to both of you."

They sprinted over to the sidelines. "What's up coach?" David asked.

"The national team has requested that I release both of you to play in a friendly match against the U.S. in a couple of weeks. I said I would on the provision that none of their activities interfere with any of our league games. Is that okay with you?"

"That's great," they both answered in unison.

The coach turned his focus to Alex. "I also said your release is dependent on the condition of your leg. How's it feeling?"

Alex had hurt the ACL of his right leg at the end of last season. The doctors had indicated it was a strain and not a tear, so they were hoping he could avoid surgery.

"It feels great," Alex said.

David knew Alex wasn't telling the whole truth. Although Alex could make it through a practice without showing any ill effects, David also knew he had to ice his knee after every practice to reduce the swelling. It was still pretty tender.

"Okay," the coach said. "But remember, the priority right now is our own game against McMaster. After that game, I'll release both of you to play with the national team, but you have to be back here the following week to play against York."

* * *

It was almost ten before Henry made it into the Chicago office of Richards, Blackwood and McTavish. He gently tapped on the open door of Sharon Robertson, the Systems Manager for the Chicago office. Henry relied on her to keep things running smoothly. Lawyers weren't known to be the most patient people in the world when computer problems arose.

"I wasn't expecting to see you here today," Sharon said. "What's going on?"

"Yeah, I only decided at the last minute to come to Chicago." He didn't share the fact that that it was his feelings of loneliness that had been the deciding factor in scheduling his trip. "What's the scuttlebutt about the merger around here?"

Henry's firm of Richards, Blackwood and Thornton had merged with the Chicago firm of McTavish & Company over a year ago. Now there were rumours of a further expansion with a New York City firm.

"Well, a few weeks ago, everyone was talking about it," Sharon said, "but now no one is talking. There's a lot of closed-door meetings and whispering in the hallways."

"That probably means they're getting serious," Henry said. "We're not hearing anything in Toronto. Do you know anything about their software systems?"

"Not much, other than they say they've got the best legal software in the country."

Henry rolled his eyes. "Every law firm says that. I'll start digging to see what I can find out. I'll probably be here for a few days this week."

"Just let me know if there's anything I can do to help," Sharon said.

Henry headed into a small meeting room down the hall. He didn't have, nor need, a regular office in Chicago, so he normally just reserved one of the meeting rooms to use during his visits. He glanced at his watch and decided to call Laura.

"Chicago Tribune – Laura Walsh speaking."

"Hi, it's just me," Henry said.

"Oh – hi. They just told me I had a call on this line but didn't say who it was. I've got someone on hold on the other line. What's up?"

"Nothing. I just never got to say goodbye before you left for work this morning, so I thought I'd call."

"That's because you fell asleep right after our little rendezvous."

"Yeah, sorry about that."

"Look, I've got someone on hold so I've got to go. I'll see you back at the condo later tonight, okay? I'll probably be quite late."

"Okay," Henry said. "Love you," he continued, but heard the click of the phone before he got the last words out.

* * *

"Hi Todd, sorry about that," Laura said when she switched back to the caller she had on hold. "We should probably stop calling each other at the office or else we'll both be in trouble."

"Yeah, that sounds like a good idea. Have you got a cell phone you can use that can't be traced?"

"Yeah, I've got one that I use when I want to talk to someone off the record." She gave Todd the number.

"Okay," Todd said. I'll pick up a burner phone and text the number to your cell."

"Sounds like a plan. Oh, you probably shouldn't come by the condo anymore. Henry's in town and getting a bit suspicious about what we're up to."

"You're not going to tell him, are you?"

"No, it's probably best to keep this between us."

* * *

Later that afternoon, Laura received a text on her cell phone. The message consisted of just a phone number, but she knew who it was from.

"Hi, it's me," she said when she called the number. "Did you find anything out?"

"A little bit," Todd said. "The documents they accidently released had to do with the Kennedy assassination."

"Who cares about that anymore?"

"Well, apparently the Secret Service and the CIA do for starters. They're tracing everyone who downloaded the documents using their IP address and then using whatever means they have to get them back. There's no shortage of money, guns and lawyers involved in this one."

"What's in the documents that they're so afraid of?"

"I have no idea, but we've been told to stay out of their way. You can't use any of this in your story. This is just background info to get you pointed in the right direction."

"Yeah, I know," Laura said. "Thanks. I'll take it from here."

Laura spent the rest of the afternoon and evening reviewing old information about the Kennedy assassination. Although it had happened about fifteen years before she was born, she knew it was a major event that affected the entire nation, and probably the whole world. It was almost midnight before she made it home.

"Long day?" Henry asked when she came through the door of her condo.

"Incredibly long," Laura said. "I just want to crash."

So much for spending some quality time together, Henry thought to himself. "Making any progress on your story?"

"A little, but not much." Laura slumped onto the couch. "How was your day?"

Henry started telling her about the potential merger with the New York firm. "There's a chance I might have to go to New York to gather some info on their computer systems. Any chance you could get away to join me? Maybe we could go to a show on Broadway or just see the sights."

He didn't get a response. He looked over to see Laura had already fallen asleep. He gently placed a blanket over her, kissed her on the forehead and then headed off to bed himself. When he awoke in the morning, she was already gone.

*** CHAPTER 6 ***

David was surprised to see a blond girl wearing very short shorts and a pink *"I Love New York"* T-shirt standing there when he opened the door.

"You David Shaw?" she asked.

"Yes," he said.

"The buildin' manager said I had to come see you to fill in some stupid questionnaire." She maneuvered her way around David and into his room. "So let's get this over with."

She was only about five feet tall and about a hundred pounds, but she looked like she could handle herself in any situation. She smelled like apples, which David assumed was her shampoo. Whatever it was, he had an overwhelming desire to smell her neck. He found his eyes drifting down to her breasts which were stretching the material of her shirt to the limit.

"You like my T-shirt?" she asked. "I bought a bunch just before I left home, but I think they shrunk when I washed them. You don't think it's too small, do-ya?"

David could feel himself blushing. "No, I think it looks

great."

"I'm Heather, Heather Low, but my friends call me Bronx." That made perfect sense. She had a very thick Bronx accent. "Don't know what questionnaire the buildin' manager wants me to complete 'cause I did one when I sent my application."

"You probably just completed the basic form," David said. "There's a more detailed one that asks a bunch of questions to help us match you with the best possible roommate."

"Whatever. Let's get this over with."

"You can use my computer," David said. Once he logged in, he found her name on the waiting list and clicked on the button to start the questionnaire. "Okay, have a seat."

"You have a roommate?" she asked. "I betcha you and I would be a good match. Then I wouldn't have to complete this stupid questionnaire."

Is she hitting on me? He wasn't used to such assertive girls. "Sorry, but I already have a roommate – my older brother."

He watched as she started the questionnaire. In fact, he found it impossible not to watch her. He noticed that she was registered in Business & Economics and wondered if she'd be in any of his classes.

"I already answered this question!" she said after a few minutes.

David could tell she was getting frustrated. "Some of the questions may appear like they're the same, but they're really not. The questions adapt based on some of your previous answers to try to drill down on your real personality by presenting different scenarios."

"Wha-da-ya' mean?"

"Let me explain," David said. "Up here you indicated you'd prefer a roommate that was neat and tidy."

"Yeah, who wouldn't?"

"You'd be surprised. Now the question down here asks whether it would bother you if your roommate didn't make her bed every day."

"Well, you don't have to be fanatical about it."

"That's my point. That really bothers some people. Further down, it asks whether it would bother you if your roommate played music while they studied."

"No," she said.

"But would it bother you if they were blasting rap music at two in the morning?"

"I hate that shit," she said.

She completed several more questions while David watched. "These questions are stupid. I thought it would just ask stuff like if I prefer to wear jammies or a night-gown to bed." She looked directly at David. "Neither, in case you're interested. Don't wear nuthin to bed."

Okay, she was *definitely* hitting on him. David felt his face flush. "I have a girlfriend – back in my home town." He thought of Ashley, the girl he had been going out with in the last year of high school.

"Is it serious?"

"Yes, but we're not engaged or anything."

"You sleepin' togetha?"

David could not believe how bold this girl was. "I don't see where that's any of your business."

She winked at him. "That would be a no then, wouldn't it? If she hasn't sealed the deal, then I consider you fair game."

David had to get up and walk away. He knew he was in way over his head.

"Done," she said a few minutes later. "When will I know who my roommate is?"

"The building manager should be able to tell you once

34

he runs the matching program, probably later today." David led her to the door.

"Can't you just click somethin' and run it now? Hate to get stuck with some preppie bitch." She reached out and traced the WLU logo on the front of David's shirt. "Maybe you could tweak it so I get the roomie I really want."

"Are all girls from New York like you?"

"Only those of us from the Bronx – and I'm one of the *shy* ones."

David found her anything but shy. "Well, Bronx seems like a really good nickname for you."

"What's your nickname?" she asked.

"Don't have one."

"Well, we can't have that. How 'bout I call you *Crush* since I have a bit of a crush on you?"

"I don't think so," David said.

"Oh, I know," she said, her eyes lighting up. "I got the perfect handle for you."

"And what would that be?"

"Goliath," she said as she walked away.

* * *

After she left, David sat on his bed in total shock for several minutes. Was she his new contact? She couldn't be. She didn't seem the type. But it couldn't just be a coincidence that she had called him Goliath, could it?

David pulled his laptop from the hidden compartment in his soccer bag. He was hoping there would be a new message telling him what to do.

"*Welcome, Goliath,*" appeared on the screen after he had logged in.

"*Retrieve instructions,*" he typed into the computer.

There was a new message. It was from a contact David had never heard of before called the *Black Knight*.

"*Watch out for the second shooter,*" was all that the message said.

David had no idea what it meant.

*** CHAPTER 7 ***

Laura hung up the phone after her conversation with another one of her insiders in the government. She headed into her editor's office to give him an update. "We're finally getting somewhere on this story."

"It's about time," her editor said without looking up. Lou fit the stereotypical image of an old-school newspaper editor. He was balding, in his early fifties, and overweight, which was not surprising since he rarely left his desk and all of his meals came in one kind of fast-food bag or another. He usually washed it down with a few quick gulps from a water bottle that sat on his desk, but everyone knew it was something other than water inside. "What have you got?"

"My source says they accidently released some of the documents related to the Kennedy assassination."

"We already knew that," he growled. "Tell me something I don't already know."

"Well, apparently some of them were ones the President had indicated should remain classified."

"What's in the documents?"

"He wouldn't say, but he did say it would prove there

was a conspiracy in the assassination. Said it would prove there was a second shooter."

Lou stopped typing and looked up at Laura. "Will he go on record with that?"

Laura knew they always lived in fear of being scooped on a big story by the TV stations or some online blogger. But they were journalists and had higher standards. They weren't always first, but they had to get it right. "No," she said reluctantly. "I can't use his name. If I do, he said he'd deny everything."

"Then you better find another source."

Laura knew he was right. "I'll keep digging."

* * *

David looked up into the stands of University Stadium and saw the brightly coloured seats of purple and gold, the colours of the Wilfrid Laurier Golden Hawks. This was their home opening soccer game against the McMaster Marauders. They always hoped for a big crowd, but there were only about two hundred people in attendance. That was probably a good thing as it was a pretty boring game, even for those on the field. The Golden Hawks were ahead two-nil and David was finding it difficult to keep his focus.

Suddenly he heard someone yell "*Go Hawks Go*" in a very thick Bronx accent. That could only be one person. He scanned the faces of the people in the stands until he locked in on her. She was carrying a sign, but David couldn't make out what it said.

He found himself thinking about her New York City T-shirt as he ran down the field – and how she smelled. How did she manage to smell so good?

David was jolted awake from his trance when the ball glanced off his shoulder and out of bounds. A teammate had passed him the ball and he hadn't even seen it coming.

"David, get your head in the game!" his coach yelled from the sidelines.

David heard a few of his teammates chuckle. They knew what he had been focused on. He could feel his face flush as he hustled back into position. He was now determined to finish out the game without getting distracted again. Sure enough, he intercepted the ball and sent a clear pass forward to one of their strikers. Unfortunately, the McMaster defender got a head on it and deflected it out of bounds along the end line.

Since they were now into injury time, this would probably be the last play of the game. The coach yelled for Alex to leave his position as defender to take the corner kick as he had the most powerful leg on the team.

"B5," the coach yelled from the sidelines.

The team had spent a lot of time on corner kicks at their last practice and the coach was anxious to see whether the work would pay off in a goal. B5 was the play where all of the forwards would move toward the front of the net and the near goalpost, but David would drift back away from the other players toward the far post.

The plan was working to perfection as all of the defenders moved forward leaving David unmarked. With Alex's leg strength, he easily curved the ball over the heads of the defenders to David.

David could have easily just tapped the ball into the open net when it came to him, but for some reason he leapt high into the air and scissor-kicked it over his head into the net. The partisan crowd rose from their seats and roared their approval.

David's teammates came over to congratulate him on his highlight-of-the-night goal, but the McMaster goalkeeper was pissed. "Fucking hot dog," he said as he pushed David to the ground. David's teammates came to his defense and there was a lot of pushing and shoving among the players until the referee got things under control. The referee called the goalkeeper over, showed him a yellow card and then waved for him to get back in his net.

Then the referee called David over and showed him a yellow card as well. "You're lucky all he did was shove you. I don't want to see any more showboating from you. Got it?"

David nodded. He knew he was right. It *was* a hot dog move and he felt embarrassed about doing it. It was okay to score and win, but it was never okay to embarrass your opponent. "I don't know why I did that."

But that was a lie. He knew exactly why he did it and she was watching him from the sidelines.

* * *

The building manager looked up from his computer to see two strangers standing in the doorway to his office.

"Can I help you?" he asked.

"I'm Officer McKee, RCMP," the first man said flashing his badge. The second man didn't identify himself, but he also looked like a police officer. "We've traced some illegally downloaded information to one of the tenants in this building. We'd like your help in identifying exactly who it was."

"I'd like to help you, but I'm not sure I can."

Officer McKee placed a warrant down on the desk and leaned in until they were almost nose to nose. "Then I suggest you find someone who can."

The building manager picked up the walkie-talkie on his desk. "Paul, can you come to my office please?"

"Give me two minutes," Paul answered.

"Paul's our telecom guy," Scott said to the officers. "I don't know much about the techie stuff, but Paul does, so

I'm sure he'll be able to help you."

He started shuffling all of the stuff around on his desk to try to make it look more organized. "You know, these kids get away from home for the first time and before you know it, they're downloading stuff from porn sites. But I don't think they're criminals, just curious kids."

"This is not about kids downloading porn," Officer McKee said.

Scott had no idea what else it could be. "So what are they downloading?"

"We're not at liberty to say."

Just then, Paul showed up. "What can I help you with?"

"These guys are from the RCMP," the building manager said, "and they're trying to figure out who's been downloading some illegal stuff off the Internet. I told them you should be able to help them."

"Maybe," Paul said. "Do you have a warrant?"

Officer McKee snatched the warrant from the desk and held it about two inches in front of Paul's face. "It's a matter of national security."

Paul looked a little skeptical.

"I'm sure we should be able to help out the RCMP," the building manager said, trying to avoid any confrontation.

"A very large amount of data was transmitted to the IP address of this building," Officer McKee said. "We simply need to know which tenant received the data."

"Our system tracks that type of information," Paul said. "I can tell you who made long distance phone calls or how many bits and bytes were sent or received from any location in the building, but I can't tell you what was in the transmission."

"We already know *the what*. We just need you to tell us *the who*."

Paul used the building manager's computer to log into

the telecom management system and started scrolling through the log files. Most were small transmissions, but one large download stood out like a sore thumb.

"Which room did that download take place from?" Officer McKee asked, looking over Paul's shoulder at the listing.

Paul flipped to another screen and was surprised to see which room it was. He paused before answering, but the officer could see the answer for himself.

"W308. We'd like to visit that room immediately," Officer McKee said.

"I can show you the way," the building manager said. He led the two officers down the hallway toward the elevator.

As Paul sat in the office, he had a bad feeling. He knew exactly who was in W308. Those two kids didn't seem like the type who would be involved in anything criminal. He wandered back down the hall toward the wiring closet wanting to do something to help them, but was at a loss as to what. But the answer suddenly appeared right in front of him in bright red letters - *In case of emergency.* He knew it would cost him his job if anyone found out, but he felt this qualified as an emergency. He looked down the hallway to make sure no one would see what he was about to do. Then he pulled the fire alarm.

* * *

Robert headed out of the building along with all of the other students. David was still at his soccer match.

False alarms had happened quite a bit over the last week and the students knew it would probably only be fifteen or twenty minutes until they were given the all-clear signal to return to their rooms.

Robert was just about to leave anyway. He was heading

over to the Coffee & Doughnuts lounge in the Math and Computer building to play *Magic*. *Magic: The Gathering* was a trading card game that Robert had become hooked on a few years earlier and he had been pleased to find out that it was a popular game with university students, and even a few professors.

The RCMP officers looked completely frustrated as the students streamed by them and out of the building. They knew there was nothing they could do to stop them.

"We should really leave the building as well," the building manager said to the officers.

"We'll take our chances," Officer McKee said. "Take us to W308."

The building manager took them up to the third floor and used his master key to unlock the outside door. The door to Robert's room was wide open, but David's was locked.

"What's in there?" Officer McKee asked.

"The other bedroom," the building manager said. "Every suite has two bedrooms and a common area." He used his master key to open the door to David's room. "We tell the students to lock their rooms, but most don't."

Both rooms looked like the typical chaotic mess found in residence with books and clothes scattered everywhere. "I want these computers searched," Officer McKee said as he pointed to the computers sitting on both Robert and David's desks. His partner used his cell phone to call headquarters to bring in some techies to conduct the search.

"Who's in these rooms?" Officer McKee asked the building manager.

"David and Robert Shaw," the building manager said. "They're brothers – seem like great kids. I find it hard to believe they'd be involved in anything illegal."

"Thanks for your help," Officer McKee said as he

shuffled the building manager from the room. "We can take it from here. We'll let you know if we need anything else." The officer did not want the building manager to know any more details about what they were looking for.

* * *

When David came out of the front doors of University Stadium, he found his distraction waiting for him. "Hi, Heather. I didn't expect to see you at the game."

"Call me Bronx – that's what my friends up here in Canada call me. How 'bout you call me Bronx and I'll call you Goliath?"

"Don't call me that!"

David felt guilty as soon as the words were out of his mouth.

"Sorry," Bronx said. "Are you super-religious or something?"

"No. Why do you want to call me Goliath anyway?"

"I dunno. I just thought it was cute 'cause of the whole David-Goliath thing. I'll just call you David from now on."

"Sorry," David said. "Didn't mean to bite your head off."

"Do-ya like the sign I made for the game? I got the picture of you in your jersey off the website."

The sign showed a picture of David kicking a soccer ball. It said "*Go #14 Go*" in bright gold letters above the picture and "*We love you*" below it, with small hand-drawn hearts all around the picture.

David sighed. "Yeah, it's great. But I already told you I've got a girlfriend back home."

"Yeah, but not a serious one."

David didn't answer.

"Do you wanna walk back to the residence together?" she asked. "I've been assigned to E106 but my roommate doesn't move in 'til tomorrow and there's not much to do."

"No, I said I'd wait for Alex. He's icing his knee so we'll be a while. You should just go ahead."

David saw her lower lip start to quiver. She turned and started walking away. As he watched her, he was filled with guilt. He'd been cold and harsh, but it had to be done. It wasn't that he didn't find her attractive. In fact, it was the exact opposite. It scared him how attracted he was to her. She made him think and do things he wouldn't normally do.

As she walked away, David saw her stuff the sign she had made for him into the huge trash can by the entrance. He was sure he'd just closed the coffin on any potential relationship with her.

The coffin may have been closed, but it wasn't nailed shut just yet.

*** CHAPTER 8 ***

David turned to see Alex hobbling towards him. "If this swelling doesn't go down overnight, I don't think I'm going to be able to go with the national team tomorrow," Alex said. The team bus was scheduled to pick up Alex, David and one other player just outside the University Stadium at 9:30 the next morning.

"I'm sure it'll be fine by tomorrow," David said, "and our game in Chicago isn't for three more days so you'll have a few days to rest. Don't forget to bring your player card and your passport. Coach said they won't let us across the border without them."

"Already got'em," Alex said, holding them up. When he reached around to put them back in his soccer bag, his leg gave out and he dropped them when he fell to the ground. David picked them up and shoved them into his pocket. Then he helped Alex back on his feet.

"Want me to call you a cab? I'm not sure how much more walking you should do on that leg."

"No, I'm fine," Alex said. "It's only a block and a half."

Rather than staying in residence, Alex was renting a

house along with four other guys. It was quite convenient – only a few blocks from the university and the soccer fields.

After David helped Alex back to his place, he walked a few more blocks to the new residence building. He was surprised to see a few hundred people gathered outside along with a couple of fire trucks.

"What's going on?" David asked the student standing next to him.

"The fire alarm went off – again – probably just another false alarm. I think this is the third time this week."

David scanned the crowd looking for his brother, but didn't see him. He could see Bronx standing about forty yards away, but he didn't think she saw him. He also saw a few guys dressed in suits in the crowd, which seemed strange. One of them was standing right in front of David and he could see the man was wearing an ear-piece like the ones the secret agents wear on TV.

David decided to call his brother to make sure he was okay. David had turned off his phone during the soccer game so it took almost a minute to start up. As soon as his phone became active, he heard the man in front of him talk into the microphone inside his suit jacket.

"His cell phone just became active. He's somewhere in the crowd. Spread out to find him."

David had the eerie feeling they were talking about him, but he had no idea why. He started backing away from the man in the suit as he tried to call Robert, but his call went straight to voice-mail. When he turned to see what the man in the suit was doing, they locked eyes.

"Got him," the agent said as he started to run toward David.

David had no idea what was going on, but his instincts told him to run. He tossed his phone to the ground and started maneuvering through the crowd. Every time he looked back, the agent was hot on his trail. He was within about ten yards of David when the agent went flying to the ground.

"Hey, watch where you're goin'," Bronx said as she fell down beside the man. Bronx made eye contact with David for a split second as she waved for him to get away. Then she turned her focus to the man on the ground. "What do-ya think you're doin', racing through here and knockin' me down?" She gave the agent a kick.

"You tripped me," the agent protested.

A crowd of people gathered around them trying to see what was going on.

"Yeah, right!" Bronx said. "I barely weigh a hundred pounds soaking wet and you expect everyone to believe I knocked you down? Someone should kick your ass!"

A few guys in the crowd immediately came to Bronx's defense. "Why don't you take on someone your own size?" one of the bigger ones said.

The agent reached into his suit jacket and pulled out his identification. "RCMP," he said to the man. "I suggest you back off or I'll have you arrested."

"Police brutality!" someone yelled from the crowd, but the man decided to back off rather than challenge a police officer.

The diversion had helped David gain an advantage, but he wasn't out of the woods yet. Being an athlete, he quickly distanced himself from his pursuers by weaving his way through the crowd at full speed, despite carrying his soccer bag. When he was away from the crowd, he cut through the numerous apartment buildings at Waterloo Place, trying to remain out of sight.

He decided he would try to make it to the Math and Computer building on the Waterloo campus as he remembered that Robert had told him he was meeting some friends at the C&D lounge that night. Robert had the ability to remain calm in times of crisis and David could sure use his brother's help right now.

Since he thought his Laurier purple and gold jacket would bring too much attention to him on Waterloo's campus, he decided to ditch it in a hedge beside one of the apartment buildings.

David hung back in the shadows alongside the building until there was a break in the traffic on University Avenue and then sprinted across the street hoping he wouldn't be seen. He thought he had made it there undetected until he heard the squeal of tires as a police car did a U-turn and started heading back in his direction.

He sprinted between the two engineering buildings heading toward the Math & Computer building. There was some kind of celebration going on at the Grad House that night and there was a large crowd of people milling around the small white building. He slowed to a walk as he thought that would make it easier to blend into the crowd. When a few of the patrons started heading off in the direction David wanted to go, he joined them.

Ahead, he could see two agents coming toward him. He was sure he would be caught. Fortunately, the path took them through a wooded section on campus called the *Peter Russell Rock Garden*. He quickly ducked behind one of the boulders and watched as the two agents walked by him and continued on toward the Grad House.

When a group of Chinese students came through the path shortly thereafter, David fell in behind them as if he was part of their group. He hoped he could easily just follow them into the Math & Computer building. However, they headed into the Quantum-Nano Centre instead and David felt it would be safer to stay as part of their group. The QNC was an impressive looking building of glass and mirrors that almost made you feel like you could see into the future.

Seeing there was an overpass connecting the QNC and MC buildings, David immediately headed toward the stairs. He was hoping the etched lines on the glass walls of the overpass would obscure his identity, but he was wrong.

"There he is," he heard one of the agents yell as he pointed out David's location.

David saw one of the agents head towards the MC building cutting off the way he wanted to go. The other agent sprinted toward the entrance to the QNC. He was trapped in a glass house with no place to hide.

He raced back into the QNC and down a long hallway of offices. Every office door he tried was locked. He could hear the agents getting closer and closer.

He needed a lucky break, and he got one. One of the office doors was unlocked. As David slowly opened the door, he could see a professor sitting at his desk staring at a computer screen that was running some kind of a simulation. As David closed the door behind him and slowly crept into the office, he realized the professor had fallen asleep.

There were two desks in the office and David tip-toed by the professor's desk and hid underneath the second. He could hear the professor's gentle snoring, so he knew he had successfully snuck by him. He could also hear the agents as they raced around the building trying to find him. Suddenly the office door flew open.

"RCMP," the agent shouted. "Identify yourself."

The man snorted and his chair banged into the desk when he was jolted awake. "I'm Professor Nigel Livingston. What is the meaning of this?"

"We're trying to locate a fugitive. Have you seen anyone?"

"Not a soul," the professor said. "I've been working here all night."

"Sorry for the interruption," the agent said as he closed the door.

David heard the agents check the other offices in the hallway and then go racing off in another direction. He didn't dare move or make a sound. He could hear the click of the keyboard as the professor resumed his work. David wondered how much longer this guy would be working before he called it a night. Hopefully not much longer – he was finding it harder and harder not to move or make a sound. To make matters worse, whoever's desk he was hiding under had some ratty old sneakers and the smell of sweaty feet was over-powering.

"I think it's probably safe to come out now," the professor said, "unless you prefer it down there under my TA's desk."

The jig was up. David crawled out from under the desk. "How long have you known I was there?"

"For quite some time now. I was just trying to calculate how long you could last down there before you passed out. Those shoes and sweaty socks have been there for the whole summer, so I'm sure they're pretty ripe by now."

"They certainly are," David said. "Why don't you just throw them out?"

"They belong to my TA and I refuse to clean up after him. It's sort of become a battle of wills between us."

"I think he's going to win," David said.

"Then you don't know me very well. You have no idea how stubborn and persistent I can be."

David studied the professor. In some ways, he reminded David of his father. "Thanks for not giving me up."

"No thanks necessary. So who are you and what are they after you for?"

"I'm David Shaw. I have no idea why they're after me."

The professor peered at David over his glasses. "Yes you do. Is it something you did, or something you've got?"

David could tell that this professor was no fool. "Probably something I've got."

"And what would that be?"

"I have no idea."

The professor once again peered at him over his glasses.

"Really, I don't," David said. "I'm just a courier. I have no idea what's in these files."

"Show me," the professor said.

David dug into his soccer bag and pulled out the microchip. "I have a computer that copied a bunch of files onto this which I'm supposed to deliver, but I'm still waiting to hear from my contact to pick this one up."

"And who's this contact supposed to be?"

"I don't know. I was just told that someone would be picking it up. And now the police seem to be after me."

"Well, let me take a look at that and we'll try to find out what's on it."

"I don't think you can," David said. "It's encrypted."

"Well, it's your lucky day son, because that's what I do. I haven't seen anything yet that I can't unlock. Why don't you leave it with me and we'll see what all the fuss is about?"

"I don't know," David said. "I should probably just hang onto it until I hear from my contact."

"Would you rather the police get it?"

David contemplated his options. He could make a run for it and hope to avoid the police – but they would take the microchip from him for sure if he got caught. Or he could take a chance and trust the professor – someone who could have already turned him in. "No," he finally said.

"I didn't think so. So why don't you leave it here with

me for safekeeping. I'm not going anywhere."

"How will I reach you when I want to pick it up again?"

"Just pop by whenever you're in the neighbourhood. As you can see, I practically live here. And if you can't get here in person, just send me an email at *Enigma* on gmail."

David handed him the microchip. He watched as the professor taped it to the back of a picture on his desk. "My wife Debbie will keep it safe. She's the one that takes care of me and looks after everything that's important. Speaking of my wife, it's probably time I headed home to her. You can stay here until you think it's safe to leave."

David watched as the professor packed up his things. "Good luck," he said as he went out the door.

*** CHAPTER 9 ***

As he left the MC building, Robert was oblivious to the events that had already occurred that night. He walked through the deserted campus back toward the residence shuffling through the *Magic* cards he had won in that night's game.

When he got to his room, he was surprised to see the door wide open and several people in it, including a technician wearing a white lab coat who was sitting at his computer. "Can I help you?" Robert asked.

"Are you Robert Shaw?" Officer McKee asked from the other side of the room.

"Yes. What's going on?"

"Where are the files you downloaded?"

"What files?"

"There's no point playing dumb with us. I'd suggest you turn everything over to us unless you want to spend a long time in jail."

"Look, I have no idea what you're talking about," David protested. "If you tell me exactly what you're looking for, I'll be glad to help."

The man who had been searching Robert's computer came over and whispered something into Officer McKee's ear. Despite the whisper, Robert heard him say "His computer's clean."

"Where's your brother?" Officer McKee said, changing his focus.

"I have no idea. He had a soccer game tonight. Maybe he's still at the stadium."

"At 11:30 at night? I doubt the game lasted this long."

Robert glanced at his watch to confirm the time. "I don't know. Maybe he went out for a beer with his teammates after the game."

"This computer's clean as well," said the other technician, the one who had been analyzing David's computer.

"I told you there must have been some mistake," the building manager said from the hallway. Although Officer McKee had told him to leave, he had been hovering around all night. "These are both good kids. I told you they wouldn't be involved in anything illegal."

"We're going to keep searching until we find those files," Officer McKee said, pointing a finger at Robert.

Robert glanced around the room. "It looks like you've already searched everywhere," he said defiantly. "I presume you have a warrant for all of this."

Officer McKee shoved the warrant into Robert's face. "Tell your brother he should just turn himself in." He locked eyes with Robert before turning to his team of investigators. "Okay guys, I think we're done for the night here."

Robert watched as they gathered up their stuff and left. He pulled out his cell phone to see that he had missed a couple of calls from his brother. When he tried to call him back, the call went unanswered. He left a voice-mail asking for David to return the call when he got the message. Robert didn't know that the RCMP were already in possession of David's cell phone.

* * *

It was about two-thirty in the morning when David decided that things were quiet enough for him to venture out of the professor's office. Rather than walk outside, he decided to use the overpasses to get from the QNC to the Biology building and then through to the Earth Sciences building. However, when he saw someone walking below glance up at him, he suddenly felt like the whole world was watching him. Although he could tell the person who'd seen him was only a student, he still felt the fear slice through him.

When he got to the Physics building, he decided to take the tunnels instead through the bowels of the Engineering Lecture Hall to the Douglas Wright Engineering Building. He remembered Robert had shown him this route one time when it was pouring outside. As he walked through the tunnels, every step he took seemed incredibly loud as it echoed off the concrete walls. If anyone was listening, they would hear him coming from a mile away. He started walking on his tiptoes. When he reached the DWE building, there was no choice now but to venture outdoors.

He slowly crossed University Avenue on his trek back to the residence. He thought it best not to run to bring any undue attention to himself. Rather than walking down the main streets, he decided to walk along Laurel Trail which ran beside the railway tracks.

When David finally got to the residence, he could see a police officer sitting in an unmarked car across the street.

"Damn," he said to himself. They were obviously watching for him there. He wondered if he could sneak into the building without the officer seeing him. As he crept along the side of the building, he noticed several rooms on the ground floor had their windows open. He thought he knew one person who would sneak him in, but he wasn't sure which room was hers.

He counted the windows as he crept along until he got to the one he wanted. "I hope this is the right room," David said to himself as he tapped lightly on the window.

There was no response, so he tapped again, this time a little louder.

"Who's there?" Bronx said as she slowly pulled back the curtains.

David could see that she had pulled back the curtains with her left hand, but had a baseball bat in her right hand. "It's me, David," he whispered. "Let me in."

Bronx put down the bat, cranked the window open as far as it could go, and pinched the latches on the inside of the screen to remove it. Although it didn't open very wide, it was big enough for David to squeeze through. He pushed his soccer bag through first and then shimmied through the opening.

"Thanks," he said as he fell to the floor. "And thanks for running interference for me earlier tonight."

"What did-ya do? Why are the cops after you?"

"It's probably better for you if I don't tell you."

"Why don't you let me be the judge of that? Maybe I can help."

She had already helped him more that anyone could expect, but he wasn't ready to tell her about the secret society and the microchip just yet. "I know you said your roommate hadn't moved in yet. I was wondering if I could hide out here until things cool down a bit."

"Just for the night. She's supposed to move in first thing in the morning, so you gotta be gone by then."

Bronx picked up the bat and David noticed it had a New York Yankees logo on it. He also noticed she was wearing a Yankee's "Jeter" jersey as a nightshirt. "I thought you said you didn't wear anything to bed."

"I lied. I was just flirtin' with ya. But I think you've made it quite clear that you've already got a serious girlfriend, so I won't be hittin' on you no-more."

"Yeah, sorry about that. I was probably a bit harsh earlier tonight."

Bronx looked away. "You can sleep on my roommate's bed. There's no sheets or nuthin, but I'm sure you can tough it out."

David headed across the hall, put his soccer bag on the floor and then threw himself onto the empty bed. It had been a long night and he was extremely tired. As he lay there, he was trying to think of his next move. He fell asleep before anything struck him.

* * *

David awoke with a start when he felt someone caressing his shoulder. "Time to rise-n-shine, sleepy head," Bronx whispered.

"What time is it?"

"It's still early. A little after seven-thirty, but I thought you'd wanna get outa here before too many people are up and about. My new roommate could show up at any time." She was still caressing his shoulder.

"You're probably right."

David noticed that she was already dressed. Once again, she was wearing an "*I Love New York*" T-shirt, although this one was baby-blue which matched the colour of her eyes. David also noticed she was sporting a large purple bruise on her arm.

"Is that from when you tackled the cop?"

"Yeah. He was a big son-of-a-bitch. He must have been packin' too cause I've got another big bruise on my side where his gun dug into my ribs." She raised her shirt to show him.

David had an overwhelming urge to kiss it better, but fought off the feeling. "Why did you help me – after I was so mean to you?"

"Cause, like it or not, I'm part of your posse and we watch out for each other. In the Bronx, you learn you can't make it on your own and you gotta watch each other's back. It's the code. You'd do the same for me, wouldn't you?"

"Absolutely," David said.

Bronx rose from the bed and tucked in her shirt. "I don't think you should be seen crawlin' out my window in the daylight. It's probably best if you just walk out the front door like a regular student."

"There was a cop parked out front last night," David said. "If he's still there, there's no way I'll get by him."

"We'll figure out a way."

When they got to the front of the building, David hung back while Bronx peered out the door to see if the cop was still there. "Piece-a-cake," she said. "Just follow my lead."

She confidently strolled out of the building and headed toward the unmarked police car. "Look at the bruise you gave me," she said to the officer. "I should probably sue you guys."

The officer got out of the car. "I'm sorry miss, but I was pursuing a fugitive."

"And I've got a bigger bruise on my ribs." Bronx lifted up her shirt – high enough to reveal the lacy bra she was wearing. Although he was an officer of the law, he was also a guy and Bronx knew exactly how to manipulate him. He didn't notice when David walked right by him and down the street.

* * *

David decided to head toward Alex's place. He knew his best friend would let him hide out there – no questions asked. But when he got there, David saw another unmarked police car parked down the street.

The sun was now up, so David knew that he would no longer be able to hide in the shadows. Just then, he saw two huge guys walk by, each carrying a duffel bag full of gear. David was only a couple of blocks away from University Stadium and he could tell that these were two football players heading off for an early morning practice. He decided that would be a good hiding place until he figured out what to do next. Since he was carrying his soccer bag, he didn't look that conspicuous so he fell in behind them.

When he got to the stadium, he sat down on a bench just inside the front entrance. He hadn't slept much the night before so it wasn't long until he dozed off.

He awoke with a start when someone yelled his name and poked him on the shoulder. "David, let's go," the man said.

It took David's eyes a few seconds to come into focus to figure out it was the coach of the national team. "Let's go," the coach said again. "The bus is outside."

David had completely forgotten they were supposed to meet at the stadium to catch the bus to Chicago for their exhibition game. "Sorry coach. I must have dozed off."

He had been wondering where he could hide until things cooled off and the solution had just fallen into his lap. As he boarded the bus, he recognized the faces of a few of the players from the Under-19 team. He watched as the coach counted the players on the bus.

"Okay, we're good to go," the coach yelled to the driver.

"Wait," David yelled. "We can't go yet. Alex isn't here."

"He's not coming," the coach said. "He called me this morning to say his knee was too swollen – said he wouldn't be able to make it. He tried to call you to let you know. Didn't you get the message?"

"Sorry coach. Guess I misplaced my phone."

David slumped back into his seat to begin the journey. He didn't know exactly where this road was going to lead him, but he knew it was better than staying where he was.

* * *

When David still hadn't shown up at the residence by dawn, Robert decided it was time to call his father.

"Hi, Robert. It's pretty early for you to be calling. What's up?"

"There's something strange going on. I think David might be in trouble."

"What do you mean?"

"The RCMP showed up at our room last night and searched our computers looking for some files they claim we illegally downloaded."

"What kind of files?"

"I don't know, but they didn't find anything. After they searched our computers, they went off in search of David. I told them he had a soccer game, but David didn't come home after the game."

"Did they arrest him?"

"I don't know. All I know is he didn't come home last night, so I thought I should call you."

Henry glanced at his watch. "Okay, I'll be on the next flight from Chicago back to Toronto. We'll sort all of this out when I get there."

After he hung up the phone, Henry turned to Laura. "Change of plans. I have to head back home."

Laura had only heard a bit of the telephone conversation. "What's going on?"

"I'm not entirely sure, but David is in some kind of trouble. I'll call you when I know more."

Henry quickly threw his clothes into a bag and was out the door in a matter of minutes. As he was in the taxi to the airport, he called Greg Blackwood, one of the lawyers in the Toronto office of their firm. Greg was a litigator and didn't practice any criminal law, but he was the lawyer Henry trusted the most.

"Hi Henry," Greg said when he answered the phone. "How are things in Chicago?"

"They're fine here, but there appears to be a problem brewing back home. I'm on my way to the airport as we speak."

"What's going on?"

"My oldest son Robert just called me to say the RCMP showed up at their residence last night and searched their computers looking for some files. They didn't find anything, but David didn't come home last night. Robert thinks he might have been arrested."

"Arrested for what?"

"I don't even know that he *has* been arrested, just that he's gone missing. Can you find out if the police have got him and what they think he's done?"

"Absolutely," Greg said. "I'll give Ray Peterson a call and find out what's going on." Ray Peterson worked in the criminal division of their law firm. Although Henry didn't know Ray very well, he knew that Greg would make sure they got some answers quickly.

As he flew from Chicago back to Toronto, Henry was filled with worry about his missing son. He had a weird feeling of déjà vu as he recalled the worry he had experienced when his brother Alan had gone missing a few years ago. Alan had died in a mysterious plane crash along with Edward Bronson, a media magnate who many people speculated was the head of some kind of secret society. It had taken the police several months to find the plane and Henry was convinced that it hadn't been an accident – all because of his involvement with that damn secret society. He reached for the air sickness bag as he suddenly felt quite nauseous.

* * *

Henry didn't realize that David was actually about 30,000 feet below his plane getting ready to cross the border into the United States. The team bus had just gone through the tunnel from Windsor to Detroit.

"Okay guys," the customs agent said as he boarded the bus. "Have your passports and your player cards ready for presentation and we should be able to get you out of here and on your way as quickly as possible."

There was a collective groan from the players. Most of them were trying to sleep and this was an unwelcome interruption.

David watched as the customs agent slowly made his way down the aisle of the bus checking the credentials of each player. David wondered whether the fact that the police were looking for him in Waterloo would somehow be flagged as he tried to cross the border. He would soon find out.

David reached into his soccer bag to pull out his passport and his player's card. When he looked at them, he was surprised to see that he had Alex's identification in his hand. It was only then that he remembered that he had picked up Alex's ID when he had dropped it after practice. He dug into his bag again and pulled out his own ID.

He had a decision to make; should he show his own ID

and risk getting arrested, or show them Alex's and hope they wouldn't notice? If he got caught, he could simply claim he had pulled out the wrong ID by mistake, which technically, was true. He decided to give it a shot.

David pretended to be sleeping when the customs agent poked him on the shoulder and asked for his passport. David barely raised his head as he passed the agent his ID. He figured it was a fifty-fifty chance as to whether the agent would even notice, because David and Alex looked quite a bit alike. The agent barely looked at David as he threw his ID back onto the seat and moved on to the next player.

David knew he had dodged yet another bullet.

* * *

Henry turned his phone on again as soon as he landed in Toronto and saw that he had a voice-mail from Greg Blackwood.

"Hi, it's Greg. Ray Peterson has confirmed that David hasn't been arrested, but the RCMP said that he is a *person of interest* in an ongoing investigation. Ray is trying to find out more about the investigation, but he's running into a lot of roadblocks. Call me when you land and I'll update you with anything else we find."

Henry felt relieved to hear that David hadn't been arrested, but it was quickly replaced with a new anxiety about where he could be. He called Greg to see if he'd found out anything further.

"I just landed. Got your voice-mail. Anything new?"

"Not much. The only thing we've found out is that the RCMP were following up on a request from the CIA."

"What would the CIA want from David?"

"I don't know, but we'll continue to dig."

After he hung up, Henry took a taxi home, hoping he'd find David there, but there was no sign of. him. Henry quickly jumped in his car to head off to Waterloo to see Robert so they could begin their search. He didn't notice the unmarked police car parked down the street. The RCMP were also hoping that David would head home. No one realized that David was exactly where he should have been – hiding in plain sight.

*** CHAPTER 10 ***

Laura knew exactly who was standing behind her looking over her shoulder before she turned around. The smell of cigarettes and scotch were a dead giveaway that it was Lou, her editor.

"Have you got anything we can use yet on that JFK conspiracy story?"

Laura had spent hours and hours going through the digitized records in the National Archives. The Assassination Records Review Board had released thousands of documents before they were shut down in 1998. In their final report, they'd complained that they hadn't been given enough time or money to complete their mandate. They had also reported that organizations like the CIA, FBI and Secret Service had obstructed their investigation, claiming some evidence had been lost or destroyed since 1963. Laura focused her search on the documents most recently added to the database.

"There's some new stuff here supporting the conspiracy theory, but nothing that confirms a second shooter was involved."

"What's the new stuff?" Lou asked.

"There's been speculation for years that the police altered the records about the rifle used in the assassination, and now there's evidence to support it."

Laura showed him the page from the Warren Commission report on her computer screen. "It says that the shots that killed Kennedy and wounded Governor Connally were fired by an Italian 6.5mm Carcano rifle owned by Oswald." She then flipped to a screen showing the report from the ballistics lab.

"Yeah, they both show the same thing," Lou said. "What's your point?"

Laura brought up the report filed by Deputy Sheriff Eugene Boone and Deputy Constable Seymour Weitzman, the first officers on the scene. "Weitzman signed an affidavit describing the weapon as a *7.65 Mauser bolt action equipped with a 4/18 scope and a thick leather brownish-black sling on it.*" She also showed him a picture of the rifle found in the building. As she zoomed in on the photo, it clearly showed a marking of *7.65 Mauser* on the barrel.

"The bastards changed the records," Lou said. "Have you found anything else?"

"No, but there are still thousands of documents to go through. But I did find something strange."

"What's that?"

"My contact gave me the count of the records that had been released to the National Archives." Laura showed him the number of records he had given her, which was well over a million. Then she showed him the number of records currently available on the website.

"There were more before," Lou said.

"Yep, just over a thousand documents have been deleted. I think those are the documents they accidently released that they're now trying to recover."

"Aren't they out there forever – in the cloud somewhere?" Lou was old-school, so he didn't understand what the term *cloud* meant or how the Internet worked. But there had been numerous stories of celebrities trying to have naked pictures of themselves removed from the Internet – without success.

"The National Archives deleted the documents from their servers as soon as they discovered their mistake – within an hour or two of when they were posted. Any links to them on search engines now just show up as broken links. It's only people who downloaded them before they were deleted that have them."

"Do we know who those people are?"

"We don't – but the CIA does. They've been seizing the computers of anyone they know who downloaded them – using the *Patriot Act* as their justification."

"Well somebody must have them," Lou said. "Find me those documents. That's what will tell us what actually happened back in sixty-three."

* * *

David sat in his darkened hotel room. He was supposed to share the room with Alex, but Alex's last minute cancellation meant he had the room to himself. He pulled the laptop out of the hidden compartment in his soccer bag.

"*Welcome, Goliath*" appeared on the screen after he had entered the complex password.

"*Retrieve instructions*," he typed. David desperately hoped there would be some message telling him what he should do, but there was nothing.

He was startled by a knock on the door. "Bus leaves in fifteen minutes," his coach yelled from the hall. Their friendly match against the U.S. National team was in a few hours.

David quickly entered *"EOT"* on the computer to end his transmission and then packed the computer back into his soccer bag. He decided it was probably best just to go to the soccer game with his teammates. Besides, he didn't know where else to go.

* * *

David sat on the bench wearing a yellow bib over his jersey, just like all of the other substitute players. His coach had already told him there wasn't much chance he would get to play in this game, but to be ready just in case. David knew the Canadians had some pretty good midfielders, so his chances of making the team weren't that great.

David glanced up at the stands and wondered if anyone was watching him. Probably not, he surmised. There were only about a hundred people watching the game, so he had time to get a good look at practically every person there. He wondered if the police were still looking for him back in Waterloo.

David turned his focus back to the game. They were well into the second half with the score tied at one apiece, but the Americans were starting to put the pressure on.

Suddenly there was a violent collision between one of the American strikers and a Canadian defender. Both players lay on the ground for several minutes.

"David," his coach yelled.

David sprang from his seat and sprinted over to his coach.

"You played defense in high school, didn't you?"

"Yeah, but that was quite a while ago. I've been playing midfield for a few years now."

"Well, it doesn't look like Adams can continue, so I'm going to put you in at right defense. Since Alex didn't make the trip, we're a little short on defenders right now."

"Whatever you need, Coach." David took off the yellow bib and sprinted onto the field.

David did some sprints and stretches as he watched the Canadian defender helped off the field. The American player who had been involved in the collision was also subbed off.

When play resumed, David found it difficult to keep up with the complicated forward attack of the Americans. Just when he had marked one player, another slipped in behind him. Fortunately, his speed allowed him to recover.

"Just hang on for a few more minutes," David said to himself. They were now into injury time and he was hoping they would be able to escape with a draw.

Suddenly, David saw the ball coming toward him up the middle and he left his man to step forward to challenge. He knew it was a mistake as soon as he did it, as the American player chipped the ball over his head to the unmarked player behind him who now had a clear attempt on goal.

David raced back to cover as he saw their goalkeeper move out to challenge the shooter. The American striker cut back toward the middle and rifled a shot toward the net. The Canadian goalkeeper dove to his left and got a hand on the ball, but it wasn't enough as the ball ricocheted high into the air continuing toward the net.

Just as it was about to enter the net, David leapt and scissor-kicked the ball away from the goal. His momentum carried him into the webbing of the net and he had to get several of his teammates to help him get untangled. But they didn't seem to mind at all. He'd saved the game.

* * *

It was about seven-thirty the next morning when David heard a knock on his hotel room door. He peered through the peephole to see that it was Assini, one of his teammates.

"Ready to head down for breakfast, super-star?" He held up a picture on the second page of the sports section showing David's heroics from the night before.

"Holy shit!" David said as he grabbed the newspaper.

"It was a great play, but don't let it go to your head," Assini said. "There's also a picture showing us untangling you from the net that's less flattering."

David read the caption underneath the picture that identified him and let out a heavy sigh.

"What's the matter?" Assini asked. "I thought you'd be thrilled."

David knew this was not good news, but put on a brave face for his teammate. "It must have been a slow news day. You go ahead for breakfast. I've got to finish packing. I'll be down in a few minutes."

* * *

Assini impatiently pushed the elevator button several times. Finally, the doors opened and he was surprised to see two big guys in suits standing in front of him.

"That's not him," the first guy said as he gave Assini the once-over.

"Have you seen David Shaw?" the second man said, blocking Assini's path onto the elevator.

"Yeah, two minutes ago. He's in his room, third from the end." He pointed down the hallway.

The two men shouldered their way by him and walked briskly down the hall. When they got to the room, the door was still partially open.

"FBI," the first man said as he slowly pushed the door open. He took one step into the bathroom on the right as the second officer moved into the main room.

"Clear," the first man said from the bathroom.

"Clear," the second man said as he opened the closet

doors.

They scanned the room looking for any trace of David, but he was gone.

*** CHAPTER 11 ***

Laura was just about to head off to work when she heard the door. "So much for our secure entrance," she mumbled to herself. No one was supposed to be able to get into the building without a key, but people campaigning in the upcoming election or selling Girl Guide cookies seemed to have no trouble at all.

"David – what are you doing here?"

"I'm looking for my Dad."

"Come in, come in," Laura said, "but he's not here. He flew back to Canada to look for you."

Laura led him into her living room. David slumped onto her couch and hid his face in his hands. "The police are after me."

"Why? What's going on?"

"I'm not supposed to tell anyone. Could you call my Dad? I ditched my phone. The police were using it to track me."

Laura picked up her phone and hit the speed-dial button. "Hi Henry, it's me. David's here and he needs you." She handed the phone to David and then headed into her bedroom to let them talk in private.

"David, I've been worried sick about you. What's going on?"

"I'm in trouble Dad. I don't know what to do."

"Robert told me the police searched your computers at school looking for some files. Did you hack into something?"

"No, not really."

"What do you mean – not really? Either you did or you didn't."

David could sense his father's anger rising. "Dad, it's complicated. I don't think you'd understand."

"Well, you better figure out a way to explain it to me." Henry tried to calm himself. "I'll help you – I promise – but you have to tell me what's going on."

David paused. "You know the secret society that Uncle Alan was a member of…"

"He was off his meds and wasn't thinking straight. I never really believed any of it. What's he got to do with this?"

"It was all true. There really was a secret society and now I'm a member of it too."

"You're what?"

"I'm sorry, Dad. We're not terrorists or anything like that. We're trying to do good things. I didn't mean to cause any trouble. But now, I seem to be in way over my head. I don't know what to do. The police are after me."

"Why?"

"I think it's because of what's in those computer files."

"Which is what, exactly?"

"I don't know. Really, I don't. All I did was package up the files and deliver them to my contacts."

"Contacts? What contacts?"

"Just other people in the group. I don't know their real

names, just their code names."

"This isn't making any sense." Henry thought for a few seconds. "Just stay there with Laura and I'll catch the first flight back to Chicago. You can explain it to me then." Henry took a deep breath. "It's okay, son. We'll sort everything out when I get there."

* * *

As he ended his conversation with David, Henry knew they were going to need a lawyer. He immediately called Greg Blackwood.

"I found David. He's in Chicago. He says he's in trouble – big trouble. I'm heading to the airport right now. Can you help us?"

"I'm on my way."

* * *

"My dad said he's going to catch the first flight back here," David said when Laura came back into the living room. "He said I should just stay here with you until he gets here. Is that okay?"

"Sure it is. Let me call my office."

Laura took the phone into the kitchen. "Something's come up – I'm going to be working from home today," she said to her editor.

"Okay, but keep working on that JFK story. I think you've got something there and I don't want anyone else scooping us on this story."

"Don't worry. I'm on it."

"I'm sorry," David said when she came back into the living room. Although she had spoken softly on the phone, David couldn't help but overhear her conversation to her boss. "I didn't mean to make you miss work, but I didn't know where else to go."

"It's no problem. I work from home all the time. Can I get you anything?"

"No, I'm fine." David slumped further down on the couch.

Laura pulled out her laptop and set it up on the large glass and silver desk in the corner of the living room. It was true; she really did work a lot from home. There were mounds of files and papers stacked on every corner of the desk. She picked up one of the piles and placed them on the floor to give her room to work.

The rest of Laura's condo looked like a photo on the cover of a Modern Homes and Gardens magazine. Everything seemed so clean, with a white leather sofa and chair, glass and silver end tables, and beige, almost-white carpet that extended into the dining area. The living room, dining room and kitchen were really just one big room divided by an island with four stools neatly pushed into place. However, the corner where her desk was located looked like a tornado had swept through the place. Laura didn't see the difference herself. It was like there were imaginary walls separating her home office from the rest of the room.

Laura sat at her desk and continued looking through the enormous number of digitized images and reports about the JFK assassination. She had found more and more evidence of a conspiracy, but nothing that indicated who was actually involved.

After a few minutes, she glanced over at David and saw that he had fallen asleep on her couch. "Poor kid," she thought to herself. "What kind of trouble could he have gotten himself into?"

Laura turned back to her work and opened the next file. It contained the statement from a lady claiming that she saw gun smoke come from behind the stockade fence on the grassy knoll at the time Kennedy was shot. On the bottom of the report, someone had handwritten "*Unreliable – Unconfirmed.*" When Laura opened the next file, it was from a man who claimed to have seen a puff of smoke from behind the stockade fence. It also had "*Unreliable*" handwritten on the report. Laura noted that the handwritten note was by the same person who had made the notation on the first report. She opened four more reports from other witnesses that said basically the same thing. All had been marked as "*Unreliable*" and "*Unconfirmed*". Another report was from a man who was on the grassy knoll who claimed to have heard a shot come from behind him. He also claimed to have smelled gunpowder.

How could the police have filed seven separate reports from witnesses claiming to have seen or heard a gunshot from the grassy knoll and have *all* of them discounted as unconfirmed and unreliable? Something fishy was definitely going on.

Suddenly David let out a yell in his sleep and began thrashing around on the couch.

Laura quickly moved over to comfort him. "David, it's okay. You're just having a bad dream."

David looked at her with wide-eyed terror as it took him a few seconds to figure out where he was. "Sorry," he said, wiping the sweat from his forehead.

"Let me get you some water."

David gulped it down. "I'm sorry. I didn't mean to freak you out."

"That's okay. You know, at some point you're going to have to stop apologizing and tell someone what's going on."

David looked like he wanted to tell her, but then reconsidered. "Maybe when my dad gets here."

He walked out onto the balcony and looked out at the beautiful view of Lake Michigan. "Dad says you're working on some big story. What's it about?"

"Are you old enough to know anything about the assassination of John F. Kennedy?"

"Only what they taught us in school. They said he was shot by Lee Harvey Oswald. That was a long time ago. Why are they still talking about it now?"

"Because it was an event that changed the world. Do you remember where you were when you heard about the 9/11 terrorist attacks?"

"Absolutely – I was in school. I remember my dad coming to pick me up, hugging me, and then taking me home. I didn't really understand what was going on, but I could tell that he was really scared."

"Well, for the older generation, everyone knows exactly where they were when they heard that Kennedy had been shot."

David remembered when they had learned about Kennedy in school, and how his teacher had tears in her eyes when she told them about how he was killed. "So why is this a story now?"

"Because the government just released a bunch of records from their investigation that they've been hiding for years."

"Why would they hide them?"

"Some people think that Oswald was set up to take the blame – that they covered up who was actually involved. In 1979, the U.S. House Select Committee on Assassinations did another investigation and indicated the first investigation was seriously flawed. They concluded there *was* evidence of a conspiracy, but not enough evidence to indicate who was involved."

"Yeah, I remember my teacher saying that," David said.

"But I still don't understand why this is suddenly coming out now."

"Because the JFK Records Act specified that all records relating to the assassination must be released this year, unless the President decides they should remain classified. He recently declassified thousands of documents, but they accidently released more than they should have, even the ones the President said should remain classified. Now the government is trying to get them back."

Suddenly there was a chirping sound as Laura's cell phone buzzed on her desk.

"Maybe that's my dad," David said hopefully. "He's probably made it to Chicago."

Laura knew it wasn't. This was the cell phone that Laura used for calls from her informants. She was sure it was Todd.

"Hi Todd," Laura said. "I can't talk right now. Can I call you back?"

"This is important," Todd said. "I just saw a bulletin come across the wire that every policeman in the city is looking for David Shaw. That's Henry's son, isn't it?"

"Yes, but I'm sure that's a pretty common name. I doubt that it's the same David Shaw."

Todd ignored her misdirection. "I know he's there. It's best if he just turns himself in. It will go better for him that way."

"Oh Todd, he's just a kid," she said as she looked at David. He had that innocent deer-in-the-headlights look on his face.

"Let me talk to him," Todd said.

Laura paused, not knowing what to do. "David," she said as she handed the phone to him, "this is a friend of mine with the FBI. He knows you're here and he wants to help."

"You called the police?" David started backing away from her.

"No, I didn't. I swear. Somehow they found out you were here. Please talk to him. I trust him and I'm sure you can too."

David paced back and forth. He knew it was pointless to try to keep running. "Can I call my dad first?"

"He wants to call his father," Laura said into the phone.

"We don't have much time," Todd said. "If I know he's there with you, it won't be long until someone else figures it out as well. Just open the door. I'm right outside."

She opened the door.

"I'm sorry, but I really think this is the best way for him," Todd said as he stepped around Laura. "Hello David. I'm agent Todd Knight with the FBI and there's a warrant out for your arrest."

"I didn't mean to do anything wrong," David said.

"I believe you," Todd said. "Why don't we all sit down and figure out where we go from here?"

Laura sat on the couch beside David and hugged him as if she were a mother bear protecting her cub. Todd sat on the leather chair facing them.

"Can I try calling my dad?" David pleaded.

"Sure," Todd said. He nodded to Laura who quickly tried to call Henry.

"It went straight to voice-mail," Laura said. "He's probably still in the air."

"I'm sorry, but I don't think we can wait for his plane to land," Todd said. "David, I think it's best if you voluntarily turn yourself in. I'll say that Laura suggested you call me because she knows me and trusts me."

"I do," Laura said, giving David a reassuring hug.

"Now David," Todd continued. "I'm going to have to put you in handcuffs, but we'll throw your coat over top so it's not too noticeable."

"Is that really necessary?" Laura asked.

"Unfortunately, yes," Todd said. "Just bring your ID with you, but I'd suggest you leave everything else here."

"And Laura," Todd continued, "I'd suggest you get one of your photographers ready at the entrance to FBI headquarters on Roosevelt Road to get a picture of us when I bring him in. You should probably leak it to some of the other media as well." He smiled at David. "We'll want a few pictures of this fresh-faced kid walking into FBI headquarters voluntarily so they can't spin some story about him being a terrorist."

"I'm sure everything will turn out okay," Laura said as she gave David another hug. Then she looked directly at Todd. "You make sure you take care of him."

She watched Todd lead David down the hallway toward the elevator. "I'll let your dad know what happened when he gets here."

* * *

Todd read David his rights as he drove him downtown to FBI headquarters. "Do you understand your rights as I have explained them to you?"

"I guess so," David answered.

Todd glanced over and could see that David was scared out of his wits. "I suggest you use those rights. Once I take you into headquarters, you're going to be placed in an interrogation room. But don't say a word until your lawyer gets there."

"Will I be able to see my dad?"

"Probably – but only briefly. Since you're over eighteen, they might only allow your lawyer to be in there with you while they question you."

David closed his eyes hoping this was all just a bad

dream.

"There's a bunch of cops feeling really embarrassed that you eluded them for so long," Todd said, "and then to have your picture show up in the paper playing in a soccer game pissed them off even more. If your lawyer is any good, he should be able to use that to his advantage. And I'll be stating that you turned yourself in."

David still just sat there with his eyes closed.

"Okay, we're getting close," Todd said. "There's going to be some reporters there so remember to just smile and look like this is just some big misunderstanding. Don't answer any of their questions."

As Todd approached FBI headquarters, he could see a couple of reporters waiting for them, along with a camera-man. Laura had obviously done her part. Todd could have easily snuck David in through a back entrance, but he wanted him to be seen with his head held high walking right through the front doors.

"Ready?" Todd asked.

"I guess so," David said.

Todd got out of the car and came around to the other side to open the door for David. He placed David's Team Canada jacket over his hands to hide the handcuffs. "Remember to smile," he whispered to David.

When they emerged from the car, both Todd and David tried to make it look like they were best buddies rather than arresting officer and prisoner.

"What are the charges?" one of the reporters asked.

David did his part and didn't say a word, but just smiled for the camera.

"Please make way," Todd said. "He's here of his own accord to answer some questions."

Todd quickly led David by them and into the building.

* * *

Laura paced back and forth in her living room, checking her watch for about the tenth time in the last five minutes. "What was taking Henry so long?" she wondered. His flight should have landed over an hour ago. Finally, her phone rang.

"It took us forever to get through customs but we're on our way to your place now," Henry said. "I've got Greg Blackwood with me, one of the lawyers with our firm. Let me talk to David."

"He's not here," Laura said. "He's been arrested."

"What? What did they charge him with?"

"Nothing, yet. Todd took him to FBI headquarters for questioning."

"Todd? How did Todd know he was there?"

"I don't know. He just did. Todd said they were going to arrest him at any minute. He said it would be best if David turned himself in for questioning."

Henry's frustration boiled over. "Just because you're getting cozy with your old boyfriend doesn't give you the right to have my son arrested!"

Laura felt like she'd been hit in the chest with a bazooka. She didn't know how to respond.

Greg signaled to Henry to give him the phone. "This is Greg Blackwood," he said calmly. "Do you know where they were taking David?"

"Todd said he was taking him to FBI headquarters on Roosevelt Road," Laura replied in a quivering voice.

"Thank you," Greg said. "We'll head straight over there." He held up the phone to pass it back to Henry, but Henry waved it away. "We'll be in touch," Greg said to Laura before he disconnected.

Greg handed the phone back to Henry. "Don't blame her. I probably would have recommended that David turn himself in as well."

"I don't trust him, not one little bit," Henry said, "and I think Laura is a little too close to him to see things clearly. He's got his own agenda. I just don't know what it is yet."

*** CHAPTER 12 ***

"Do you know what the prof's talking about?" a girl whispered to Robert as she nudged his shoulder.

Robert was sitting in the lecture hall of his second-year calculus class, but his mind was elsewhere. His dad had called him just before class to say that David had been arrested in Chicago. Robert wanted to head there to support his brother, but he had been told there wasn't anything he could do.

"Sorry," Robert said to the girl. "I wasn't really paying attention."

The class ended a few minutes later and Robert found the same girl waiting for him in the hallway. She was tall and athletic looking, with short brown hair. Robert didn't remember seeing her before, but there were a lot of new faces this term as the other stream of co-op students were back on campus.

"Hi, I'm Vanessa," she said as she approached him. "There's a few of us planning to meet in the lounge later this afternoon to organize a study group for this class and I was wondering if you wanted to join us."

"I don't know," Robert said. "I've got a lot on my plate right now, so I'm not sure I have the time. Sorry."

Robert started walking toward his next class, but Vanessa hustled alongside him trying to keep up with his quick pace. It was obvious she wasn't going to give up easily. "Look, there's a few of us that are going to fail this class for sure unless we work together. I was asked to recruit you into the group because we were told that you're a bit of a brain when it comes to calculus. We could sure use your help."

Robert stopped and looked at her. "And what do I get out of this arrangement?"

"Whoa buddy. We're just after you for your brains, nothing else. I can't believe you'd think I would... never mind. Forget I asked." She turned and started to walk away.

Robert felt his face flush when he realized what she thought he was looking for out of this arrangement. "Wait," he said as he hurried after her. "That's not what I meant. I wasn't asking you to – I mean, I didn't mean to imply that you should – look, I'm sorry." He was now just stammering and not making any sense at all. He took a deep breath. "I was just trying to say that if I helped you and your friends out with calculus, maybe you could help me out with one of my weaker subjects, like statistics."

Vanessa still looked suspicious of his intentions. "We're meeting in the C&D lounge at six-thirty tonight. Come if you like."

* * *

David was sitting in the interrogation room by himself, but he was starting to feel more and more relaxed. Todd had removed the handcuffs before he left and another FBI agent had asked him if he could get him some coffee. Since

David wasn't much of a coffee drinker, the agent had offered to get him a Coke from the little confectionary downstairs. A female FBI agent had popped in to ask him about his soccer game as she had seen David's picture in the newspaper. She spoke to David for about ten minutes, telling him that her son was a soccer player as well and played for the University of Michigan. Everyone was friendly and continually asking him if there was anything they could get him.

There was a sharp rap on the door and a tall, much older and scarily thin man entered the room. The atmosphere changed instantly as this man gave off the vibe of a grave digger. "I'm Tom Schwartz. I'd like to ask you a few questions."

This guy didn't look at all like the other agents David had encountered. "Are you with the FBI?"

"No, I'm with another branch of the government," he said, without any further explanation. "Where are the computer files you downloaded?"

David took a deep breath. "I'd like to wait until my dad and my lawyer get here before answering any questions."

"I'm sure they'll be here shortly, but I suggest you answer my questions if you don't want to spend a very long time in jail. You know, there are guys in prison who look forward to the arrival of fresh-faced kids like yourself." He squinted his eyes at David. "They always look forward to the arrival of fresh meat."

David's mouth suddenly went dry and he tried to remove the top of the Coke bottle to take a sip, but his hands were shaking too much. "I didn't do anything wrong. I just copied the files onto microchips like I'm supposed to and then sent them to my contacts."

"Give me their names and addresses."

"I don't know their names. I only know their code

names. I just deliver the microchips to where I'm supposed to. I don't know what happens after that."

Schwartz pushed a pad of paper in front of David, pulled a pen from his suit pocket, and placed it on the pad of paper. "Why don't you just write down their code names and the locations you delivered the microchips to and we'll see what we find?"

David wrote down the code names of his six contacts. He paused at the end, unsure whether to tell him about the microchip he had given to the professor at the university. He decided not to.

"Where's the computer you used to make the microchips?" Schwartz asked.

Suddenly there was a knock on the door. "His lawyer's here," an FBI agent said as he opened the door.

"David, don't say another word," Greg Blackwood said when he entered the room.

David saw his father in the doorway behind Greg. "Dad!" He scrambled from his chair and ran to hug him.

"What is he being charged with?" Greg asked.

"Nothing, yet," Schwartz answered. "But you'll find out all of the charges at his arraignment."

Schwartz rose from his chair and left the room, closing the door behind him. "Find that computer," he said to the two agents who were waiting outside.

* * *

Robert headed into the C&D lounge about twenty after six that evening, but there was hardly anyone there. It was called the C&D lounge because the student council sold fresh coffee and doughnuts there to raise money. Unfortunately, they had already closed up operations for the day so Robert, who hadn't had supper yet, was forced to purchase something from one of the vending machines.

The *Best Before* date on the package had faded to the point of being unreadable which caused Robert some concern, but not enough to forego what was inside the package. He flopped down on one of the couches in the lounge.

A few minutes later, a couple of students wandered in. "Are you here for the calculus study group?" one of them asked Robert.

"I guess so," he answered.

Shortly thereafter, a few more students arrived, but Vanessa still hadn't shown. Robert seriously considered bailing.

"Sorry I'm late," Vanessa said as she raced into the lounge along with another student. She was about to sit beside Robert on the couch, but when she saw who it was, she decided to sit on the couch facing him.

"Okay, we're here to try to form a study group for second-year calculus," she said. "We're not planning to do any studying here tonight, just come up with some days and times when we can get together. I've already spoken to a few of you about your availability and it appears that Monday and Thursday evenings work best, starting at six-thirty. Can everyone make it at those times?"

"Can we start at seven instead of six-thirty?" Robert asked. "I won't have time to grab supper if we start that early."

There was a murmuring of agreement to start at seven.

"And can we make sure we're done on Thursdays by eight-thirty?" Robert asked again. "I play *Magic* starting at nine."

Everyone nodded their agreement.

"Okay, does anyone else have any constraints?" Vanessa asked the group, although she was looking directly at Robert when she asked. No one else had any time constraints. "Okay, we'll have our first study group meeting this Thursday at seven here in the lounge. See you then."

Everyone started gathering their belongings and heading out. Robert headed over to speak to Vanessa. "I'd like to apologize again for any misunderstanding earlier today."

"That's okay. I guess I was partly to blame for thinking you had an ulterior motive. I've always been a little suspicious of people – not sure why." Vanessa continued loading stuff into her backpack. "But I have to ask you one more thing."

"Shoot," Robert said.

"What the hell is *Magic*?"

"You've never heard of it? *Magic: The Gathering* – it's a trading card game."

"You are *such* a nerd," Vanessa said, shaking her head.

"Well, after our study group session on Thursday, you can come to our game and give it a try. I'll even loan you some of my *Magic* cards. What do you say?"

She looked at him and smiled. "Okay."

Robert watched her as she walked out of the lounge. He found her intriguing.

*** CHAPTER 13 ***

Laura paced back and forth in her living room. It had been several hours since she'd spoken with Henry and she hadn't received any further updates. She had called Henry several times and left voice-mails, each time apologizing for letting Todd take David into custody, but in her heart she still felt it was the right thing to do. She just wished he would call her back and let her explain things.

Suddenly her phone rang and she grabbed it before it even finished the first ring.

It was Lou, her editor. "We're going to run your first story about the JFK assassination in tomorrow's paper – the one about the misidentification of the gun."

"I haven't finished going through all of the files yet," Laura protested. "I think there's more there."

"I'm counting on that. We're going to publish it as a series of articles. The first story will be about the gun. It will tie in nicely with the picture of the kid they just arrested."

"We don't even know if the two stories are related. I don't think he knows anything. He's just someone who

91

stumbled into a mess of trouble."

"Yeah, I figured that. But he's now the face of this story – a fresh-faced kid going up against a government that's trying to hide something."

"He's not even American," Laura said. "He's Canadian."

"Even better – tomorrow we're going to run the picture along with your story. The next day we'll run your story about how they discredited the witnesses who said they heard a shot come from the grassy knoll."

"That's all I've got so far."

"Then you better get cracking. We've got to stay ahead of this story." He hung up before Laura could offer any more objections.

Laura headed back over to her desk and began searching through the digitized records, concentrating on those recently added to the National Archives. After about an hour, she came across a statement from a man named Gordon Arnold who claimed to have filmed the President's motorcade that day as it made its way through Dealey Plaza. He said two policemen had confiscated his film as evidence shortly after the incident. Laura searched the database for any other records under that name, but didn't get any hits. If the statement from Mr. Arnold was correct, there was no record of his film ever being logged into evidence.

The best photographic evidence of the assassination was the now famous Zapruder film, but there were accusations that the Zapruder film had been altered – and they were right. When he sold the film to Life Magazine, Zapruder had requested that the frame showing the President's head being blown apart be withheld from the public because he thought it would be too upsetting.

Even the version that was shown to the Warren Commission was not complete. Frames 208 to 211 were missing, a splice was visible in frames 207 and 212, frames 314 and 315 were switched, and frame 284 was a repeat of frame 283. In reply to a 1965 inquiry, the FBI's J. Edgar Hoover indicated frames 314 and 315 were switched due to a printing error. In 1967, Life Magazine released a statement that four frames of the camera original (208–211) had been accidentally destroyed, and the adjacent frames damaged by a lab technician. Conspiracy theorists had suggested some frames had been altered to create confusion as to whether the final shot had really come from behind the President.

Laura continued her search and found a statement from Beverly Oliver who also claimed to have been filming that day. She said she had been contacted at work and turned over her film to two FBI or Secret Service agents who promised they would return it to her within ten days, but she never heard from them again. Using cross referencing, Laura figured out that Beverly Oliver was better known as the "*Babushka Lady*", who is shown in the Zapruder film as filming the motorcade from a different angle. Once again, there was no record of her film ever being logged into evidence.

If there was a common theme to this whole case, it was that evidence seemed to have a habit of disappearing.

Laura was interrupted when her phone rang. "Hello," she said, hoping it was Henry finally returning her call.

"Hi, it's Sam." Samantha was Laura's best friend and had been since childhood. They were like two peas in a pod and never too far apart. After high school, Laura had enrolled at Ohio State because Sam had been accepted there, and when Laura got a job at the Chicago Tribune, Sam found a job there as well within a few months. "I didn't see you at work today. Are you sick?"

"No – just working from home."

Sam immediately sensed that Laura wasn't telling the

whole story. "What's wrong?"

"Nothing. I was just hoping this call was from Henry."

Sam knew all about Henry. She had been there when Laura had met him at the bar at the Chicago airport. She had initially thought it was a bad idea for them to hook up but since then, she had come to see how good they were together. "Why? What's going on? Did you guys have a fight?"

"No, not really. He's just pissed because I let Todd arrest his son."

"What? Holy shit! I need details, girl. I'm on my way over."

"I'm fine. You don't have to come over."

"I was just about to leave work anyway. I'm on my way."

* * *

It seemed like no time at all until Sam was at her door. "Okay, spill it," she said as she waltzed by Laura and headed straight to the kitchen. Sam was tall and thin with naturally blond hair, a rarity since most women's blond hair simply matched the colour on the bottle from which it came. She had gone through a slew of boyfriends over the years, something that was starting to concern her now that she was over thirty-five. She had never met "*the one*", so she was starting to doubt he even existed.

Sam pulled two wine glasses from the cabinet, grabbed a half-full bottle of white wine from the fridge, and filled their glasses almost to the rims.

"There's not much to tell," Laura said as she took a healthy sip from her wine glass.

Sam looked unconvinced. "Bullshit."

Laura explained how David was in some kind of trouble and had come by her place looking for his father. Henry had told her to take care of him until he arrived, but then Todd had shown up to arrest him.

"How did Todd know he was here?"

"I don't know," Laura said. "Henry asked the same question." She took another sip of wine. "I think he might be a bit jealous of Todd."

"Well, duh."

"What do you mean?"

"How could he *not* be jealous of Todd? He's your old boyfriend and he hangs around you all the time. And he's got a body that any woman with a pulse would want to *do* in an instant."

"He's not around that much," Laura protested. "We're just friends and he's helping me with some research for a story."

Sam shook her head in disbelief. "He always seems to be helping you with something. Face it – the guy's still got a thing for you. The big question is whether you've still got a thing for him."

"Absolutely not," Laura said. She was tired of playing defense and decided a little offence was called for. "And when you said any woman with a pulse would want to *do* Todd, does that include you?"

"Because we're friends, I'm not going to answer that."

They glared at each other until Sam looked away.

"Look," Sam said. "All I'm saying is that if you're really interested in patching things up with Henry, you're going to have to give up whatever's going on between you and Todd."

Laura finished her wine in one big gulp. Sometimes best friends were a big pain in the ass. But sometimes they were the only ones willing to tell you what you really needed to hear. "Will you help me patch things up with Henry?"

"Of course I will," Sam said as she gave Laura a hug.

"So, if you're going to end things with Todd, does that mean that I could..."

Laura broke their hug. "Don't even think about it."

Sam could not hide her grin. "Too soon?"

*** CHAPTER 14 ***

Laura quietly slipped into the back of the courtroom and scanned the room looking for Henry. She had arrived early hoping to talk to him before David's case was called. She deliberately sat away from the other reporters in the room and placed her coat on the seat beside her to hold it for him. But it was actually Todd who plopped down beside her.

"We have to talk," Laura whispered to him. "It's probably best that we not sit together. I'll find you after the proceedings."

"That doesn't sound good," Todd whispered back. "What's up?"

"Not now," Laura said as she waved him away.

But it was too late. Henry walked into the courtroom at that exact moment and saw them together. You could almost hear the grinding of his teeth as his jaw clenched.

* * *

"Accused is to be remanded into custody. Bail set at ten thousand dollars," Judge Raymond Prowse said as he slammed down his gavel. He was presiding over arraignment court and had already quickly ruled on several cases that morning. This court was not for a formal trial; it was simply where the prosecution specified the charges being laid, the defendant entered an initial plea, and bail was set. It was also the first opportunity for the defense to challenge whether there were enough grounds to even lay charges.

Judge Prowse was a seasoned veteran so the steady stream of assault, burglary and drug charges that he'd encountered so far that day were hardly challenging his legal mind. "Next case," the judge said.

"David Charles Shaw," the bailiff announced.

"What are the charges?" the judge asked without looking up.

"Charges are for Unauthorized Computer Access, Theft and Possession of Stolen Property, Illegal Entry and Resisting Arrest," the prosecutor said.

The judge looked over his glasses at the fresh-faced kid who stood before him facing these charges. Something didn't seem right. "How does the defendant plead?"

"Not guilty," Mike Nethercott said. Mike was a criminal lawyer with the firm's Chicago office – in fact, the only criminal lawyer in the firm as they didn't practice much criminal law at all. He was in his mid-twenties and the shuffling of the papers in his hand showed his nervousness.

Beside him stood Greg Blackwood. Greg was a civil litigator and didn't practice any criminal law whatsoever, but his many years of experience had taught him how to handle himself in a courtroom. "We'd like to dispute these charges, Your Honour," Greg said. "We have a sworn statement from FBI agent Todd Knight that our client turned himself in voluntarily."

"Objection," the Prosecutor said. "Mr. Blackwood is a

Canadian and is not licensed to practice law in the United States. He may not be familiar with how we do things on this side of the border and since we want to ensure that the defendant is given a fair trial, we request that Mr. Blackwood not be allowed to represent Mr. Shaw in this matter."

"Your Honour, I thank the Prosecutor for his concern about my client, but I have been practicing law for over twenty years. I have just written the Bar exams for the state of Illinois and I expect to be licensed shortly. Mr. Nethercott is lead counsel. I am simply here as an advisor."

The judge looked closely at Mr. Blackwood and had an immediate sense that this man knew the law. "Overruled," the judge said. "Mr. Blackwood, you will not be allowed to represent Mr. Shaw at trial until you are licensed by the state, but I think we can allow you to act in an advisory capacity at this stage."

The judge turned his focus to the Prosecutor. "Is it true Mr. Shaw turned himself in voluntarily?"

"Technically, yes," the Prosecutor said. "But the defendant snuck across the border and has been evading arrest on both sides of the border."

"My client came across the border on a bus along with the rest of his Team Canada teammates," Greg said, "and played a soccer game in front of a few thousand fans. In fact, he had his picture appear in the sports pages of the Chicago Tribune." Greg held up the newspaper so the judge could see the picture. "I'd hardly describe that as a person who snuck across the border and resisting arrest, Your Honour."

"I would tend to agree," the judge said.

"Our Customs and Border Protection Agency shows no record of Mr. Shaw entering the United States," the Prosecutor said.

"If the prosecution wants, I can obtain statements from his coaches and the rest of his teammates that my client was on that bus," Greg said.

"I don't think that will be necessary," the judge said. "It wouldn't be the first time our cracker-jack border agents missed something. I'm going to dismiss the charges of Resisting Arrest and Illegal Entry into the U.S."

"I'd also like to dispute the charges of Unauthorized Computer Access and Theft and Possession of Stolen Property," Greg said.

"On what grounds?"

"On the basis that nothing was stolen, Your Honour. The government accidently made some information available on their public website for anyone to access. They are charging my client with the theft of information that they, themselves, released. He did not hack into their website to obtain it."

"Is that true?" the judge asked the Prosecutor.

"Technically, yes," the Prosecutor said.

The judge rolled his eyes in frustration. "What's really going on here?" he asked the Prosecutor.

"Your Honour, even though the information was accidently released, that does not give the defendant the right to keep that information."

"Your Honour," Greg countered, "if the government left their barn door open and their cows wandered off, that doesn't give them the right to charge my client with stealing their cows."

"Correct," the judge said. "But it also doesn't give your client the right to keep the cows. What exactly is in this information?"

"We're not at liberty to say," the Prosecutor said, "for national security reasons."

"I had a feeling you were going to say that," the judge

said.

The judge looked down at David and could see that he was just a kid who was in way over his head. "Son, do you still have this information?"

"I don't think so," David said.

"We believe the information is on his computer, which we have yet to locate," the Prosecutor said.

"Alright, let's see if we can solve this problem without anyone getting hurt or going to jail," the judge said. "Mr. Blackwood, is your client willing to turn over his computer to the government if these charges are dropped?"

Greg looked briefly at David and could see in his eyes that he just wanted this nightmare to be over. "Yes, Your Honour. Those terms are acceptable to us."

"Mr. Blackwood, please ensure that your client turns the computer over to the Prosecutor within twenty-four hours." The judge then looked directly at David. "Son, I'd recommend that you do that immediately and then get yourself back to Canada as soon as possible. If I see you here in my courtroom again, I doubt things will go as well for you next time."

"Yes sir," David said with his voice starting to crack.

"Case dismissed," the judge said as he pounded his gavel. "You are free to go."

Henry leapt from his seat and raced up to hug David. "Thank God," he said as he almost sucked the air out of him. "Where's the computer they're talking about?"

"It's at Laura's condo, in my soccer bag."

Henry locked eyes with Laura and everyone in the room could feel the tension.

"Why don't you take David straight to the airport?" Greg said. He knew that this was not the time or place for them to resolve their issues. "I'll make arrangements to get the laptop from her and turn it into the Prosecutor and then

I'll just meet you at the airport with David's bag."

"Thanks," Henry said as he locked arms with David and led him out of the courtroom.

Laura tried to shuffle her way by the people in front of her to catch them before they left, but Henry and David were gone by the time she got out into the hallway. She found Greg Blackwood waiting for her along with a detective.

"I just wanted to talk to Henry to explain," Laura said in frustration.

"I know," Greg said, "but I think it's best to just let him cool down a bit first. I've already told him that I would have recommended that David turn himself in as well, so you didn't do anything wrong. I think Henry will eventually see that."

"I just need to see him."

"First things first," Greg said. "This fine detective here has kindly agreed to drive us to your place so we can retrieve David's laptop."

As they sat in the back of the detectives' car on their way to her condo, Laura kept trying to explain to Greg what had happened. But each time, Greg raised his finger to his lips and nodded towards the detective who was watching them through his rearview mirror. "We'll talk later," Greg whispered to her.

When they got to her condo, Laura retrieved David's soccer bag and gave it to Greg. He pulled the laptop from the hidden compartment at the bottom of the bag and handed it to the detective. "I'd like a receipt for that and would like it returned to my client as soon as possible."

As the detective wrote the receipt, Greg did a quick search through the rest of the contents of the bag. He saw the two Canadian passports, one for David and one for another soccer player. He had a sneaking suspicion as to how David had crossed the border undetected and quickly closed the bag.

"Thank you," Greg said to the detective when he handed Greg the receipt. "I believe you have everything you require."

Greg waited for the detective to leave before he spoke to Laura. "I should be getting to the airport so I can get David back home safely. I'll talk to Henry on your behalf and try to convince him that what you did was in David's best interest."

"Just tell him that I …," Laura said before Greg cut her off.

"I'm sure he already knows, but I'll leave it to you to deliver that message personally."

* * *

The detective sat in his car as he watched Greg Blackwood get into a taxi and head to the airport. He pulled out his cellphone and made a call, but it wasn't to headquarters. "I have the laptop. What do you want me to do with it?"

"Bring it to me before you turn it into evidence," the person on the other end of the phone said. "I want to find out how much that kid knows."

"Do you want me to follow him to Canada?"

"That won't be necessary. We've already got someone watching him and his brother."

*** CHAPTER 15 ***

As David, Henry and Greg flew back to Canada, David explained to his father how he had become involved in the secret society. Although they were whispering to each other, Greg was still nervous that the other passengers sitting around them could overhear. "I'd recommend you wait until you get back home to talk."

When the taxi pulled into their driveway, David was surprised to see several family members waiting for him. Robert had come home from university after he'd received the call from Henry saying they were on their way back from Chicago. His aunt Jenny and his grandmother were also there.

"I guess I owe you all an explanation," David said.

"You don't owe us anything," his grandmother said as she hugged him. "I'm so glad that you're home safe and sound."

They all headed into the house and gathered in the living room. Everyone except grandma that is, who seemed more intent on making sure they all had something to eat and drink.

"First of all, I'd like to apologize to all of you." David said.

"I'm not exactly clear on what you're apologizing for," Robert said. "What did you do?"

"It's sort of complicated. It's probably best that I start at the beginning. It all started a few years ago, before Uncle Alan disappeared. Uncle Alan told me that he was part of a secret society and he asked me to carry on if anything should happen to him."

"Why would you agree to anything like that?" his Aunt Jenny asked. "You knew he wasn't thinking clearly."

"Yeah, I thought so at first too. Dad told me about his bipolar condition, so I thought this was just one of his fantasies. But the more we talked – I had a feeling that it wasn't all just in his head. When his plane disappeared and those RCMP officers showed up asking about his code name and the group he was involved with, it appeared that it was all true."

"His code name?" Robert asked. "Uncle Alan had a code name?"

"Goliath," Henry said. "Alan told me that he was Goliath, but I didn't believe him. He'd been off his medications for a few days."

"I remember that day," Robert said. "He showed up here acting like he was some kind of a rock star. But I still don't understand how you got involved."

"Remember the break-in at the house?" David said.

"How could I not?" Robert answered. "It scared the shit out of me. I came home and found two guys rummaging through our house. They went out the front door when I came in through the back. But the only thing they took was Uncle Alan's laptop."

"Actually, I'm the one who took the laptop," David confessed. "I was worried the police were going to take it, so I hid it in my soccer bag before they came back with a search warrant."

"How did you get it to work?" Robert asked. "It was password protected. Dad and I tried to hack into it but we couldn't get past the encryption."

"Uncle Alan had given me the password. I've been using it ever since. Or I was, until they just took it from me in Chicago."

"Okay, I'm missing something here," Aunt Jenny said. "Are you saying that Alan was a spy and that now you're one too?"

"Not spies," David said. "We're just members of a secret society."

"A secret society that does what?" Jenny asked.

Henry's ears perked up at this point. David had told him about the code name and the laptop on their flight home, but he had no idea what this secret society actually did.

"It's hard to explain," David said. He could tell that it all seemed so unbelievable. No wonder they all thought his uncle Alan had gone nuts. "The group was started by Edward Bronson."

Edward Bronson was a very rich media magnate that owned several newspapers and TV stations in Canada. It was his plane that crashed, killing both Alan and himself. The police suspected the plane had been tampered with, but had never proven anything.

"He believed that our most important problems would never be solved by politicians," David said. "But he believed that these problems *could* be solved if we got the smartest people working together on solutions. The key was that it had to be anonymous. No one would be able to patent the idea or profit from the solution. No one would get to take credit for the solution to get elected. People would want to be involved, not for money or fame, but simply because it was the right thing to do."

David looked around and could see the skepticism on the faces of his family. "I know it sounds like a pipe dream, but that's why I agreed to be part of it. I'm so frustrated with our current political structure. If one party proposes a solution, then the other one is immediately against it, regardless whether it has any merit or not. All the political parties are more interested in getting elected than they are about making any real progress."

"I think we all share your frustration with politics," Jenny said, "but I still don't really understand what you do as part of this secret society."

"I'm just a courier," David said. "When information is sent to me, I'm supposed to distribute it to my contacts. And then they distribute it to people who have the skills to actually solve the problem."

"So why did they arrest you?" Jenny asked. "This doesn't sound like something that would be illegal."

"I'm not sure," David said. "I think the American government might be trying to hide something. I didn't look at any of the information, but I think it's some kind of a cover-up."

"Well, I think we've heard enough about secret societies for today," Henry said. "David is back safe and sound and we're all grateful for that." Henry had decided the secret society had caused enough trouble for the family. "This family's involvement in secret societies is over."

"Why would he stop?" Grandma said from the kitchen. She had been listening to everything as she brought them all something to eat and drink.

"Mom, you don't understand," Henry said.

"I think I do," she protested. "It sounds to me like this group is trying to accomplish something worthwhile. Why would he stop now?"

"Because it almost got him sent to jail."

"That's no reason to stop," she said. "Alan knew it was worthwhile – that's why he asked for David's help. And David, I can see that you believed in it. Has that changed?"

David looked at his grandmother and could see the fire in her eyes. "No - not really. But I don't want to go to jail either."

"Sometimes you have to be willing to go to jail to fight for the things you believe in. Your grandfather went to jail fighting for workers' rights. We fought against our own government until they brought in proper health care for all of us, and not just for the rich." She quickly picked up the various dishes and cups from the coffee table, took them back into the kitchen and slammed them into the dishwasher. "You do what you think is best."

David had no idea what he was going to do.

*** CHAPTER 16 ***

Just after supper that night, there was a knock on the front door.

"Ashley, it's good to see you," Henry said as he opened the door. "David's in his room."

Ashley was David's girlfriend. They had both played on their high school soccer teams and had been going out for a little over a year. Ashley was a year younger than David, so was still in high school.

Ashley took a quick look at herself in the mirror just inside the door and quickly fluffed up her short brown hair before heading down the hall toward David's room. His door was half-open and she could see him lying on the bed staring at the ceiling. "Knock, knock, knock," she said as she gently pushed the door open.

"Ashley! I'm so glad to see you."

"How's my little fugitive doing?"

"I don't even want to think about that anymore," David said as he pulled her onto the bed beside him. "Just lie here with me for a bit."

They lay on the bed hugging each other for several

minutes without saying a word. "You know, one of the things I like best about you is that I feel so comfortable when I'm with you," David finally said. "No pressure, no stress. It's like you're my very own security blanket."

Ashley scrunched up her nose. She wanted to be perceived as something more exciting than a security blanket, but she let it go. "I'm so glad you're back. Are you going to stay home for a few days?"

"No, Dad's driving us back to Waterloo later tonight."

"I was hoping that you'd be able to stay for a while. We hardly see each other. I hate being in a different city than you."

"Me too, but I've already missed several days of classes. I can't afford to fall too far behind."

"Do you have to worry any more about the police?"

"I don't think so," David said. "I think the stress of that whole ordeal is all behind me now."

* * *

As Henry drove his sons back to Waterloo that night, there wasn't a lot of conversation. Robert kept asking David questions about getting arrested, but David kept saying he didn't want to talk about it.

"Just leave him alone for a while," Henry said to Robert. "It was pretty scary for him. I'm sure he'll talk about it when he's ready."

"Are you still going to be a member of the secret society?" Robert asked, ignoring the request for silence.

"I don't know."

"Well, Grandma sure thinks you should be."

David was getting more and more frustrated. "I said I don't know!" He pulled the hood of his sweatshirt over his head and slumped down in the backseat so he wouldn't have to answer any more questions. But his grandmother's comments *had* struck a nerve. In his heart, he still believed in the society and their goals. He just wasn't sure he was willing to pay the price to pursue those goals. He was sure his Grandma would be disappointed in him. Hell, he even felt a little disappointed in himself. He didn't want to be the kind of guy who could be intimidated, but that's exactly what had happened.

Robert was about to ask another question, but Henry poked him and the look on his face told him it was time to drop it. They drove the rest of the way in silence.

* * *

Once they got to the residence, David went to his room and was trying to get organized for classes the next day. Robert had just plopped himself down in front of the TV when there was a knock on their door.

"If that's for me, I'm not here," David said from his bedroom.

Robert opened the door and saw a short blond girl standing there.

"Hi, I'm Bronx," she said. "I was wonderin' if you'd heard anythin' from David yet?"

Robert was just about to turn her away when David poked his head out of his room.

"David!" Bronx said as she burst by Robert and raced toward David. She leapt into his arms, wrapping her legs around his waist and gave him a big kiss on the cheek. "I'm so glad you're safe. I was *sooo* worried about you."

"I'm fine," David said, looking extremely embarrassed.

"Sorry 'bout that," Bronx said as she wiped her pink lipstick from his cheek. "I know, I know, you've already got a girlfriend. But I'm so glad you're back. I thought I was going to have to visit you in prison."

"So you heard about my little adventure."

"Only what they said in the newspaper."

David looked up to see that Robert was still standing by their front door. His eyes and mouth were wide open.

"Uh, Bronx," David stammered, "this is my brother Robert. Robert, this is Bronx."

"Yeah, I got that," Robert said, but he was still surprised by what he had just seen.

"I helped Bronx answer the roommate questionnaire a few weeks ago."

"Uh-huh," Robert said, waiting for more.

David just gestured with his palms up, not knowing what else to say.

"So tell me what happened?" Bronx asked. "And don't leave nuthin out." She pulled David over to sit on the loveseat.

"I guess I'll just head to my room," Robert said. He wasn't sure either of them heard him, or cared.

"Well, after I hid out at your place, I tried to head over to Alex's place but there were cops there so I just hopped on our team bus to Chicago," David said. "I thought for sure they'd get me at the border, but I used Alex's passport to sneak across."

Robert was in his room listening to everything. David wouldn't tell him a thing, yet here he was telling this girl everything.

"I thought things might calm down after a few days," David continued, "but the FBI figured out where I was and arrested me."

"The paper said you turned yourself in."

"Yeah, that's true. But that's only because Laura – that's my dad's girlfriend – knows an FBI agent."

"So what did you steal?"

"I didn't steal anything. All I did was transfer some files. I don't even know what was in those files, but I think it's some kind of government cover-up."

"No shit. So, you're like some kinda super cool spy?"

David was running on adrenalin now. He liked how Bronx was looking at him – like he was a super hero. Then he suddenly realized he had probably said way too much. "Not really," he confessed.

"Were you scared?"

David recalled how scared he was when he was in the interrogation room. "A little bit." He didn't want to reveal to Bronx how scared he really was.

"Are they going to send you to jail?"

"No, my dad's lawyer got them to drop the charges, but I had to give them my computer."

"So what happens now?"

"Nothing." He could sense that Bronx wanted the adventure to continue. "Look, I probably shouldn't have told you as much as I did. You can't tell anyone anything that I've told you."

Bronx put her fingers to her mouth and gestured like a zipper closing between her lips.

"I'm serious," David said. "This has to remain a secret."

"Don't worry. Remember, I'm part of your posse and we watch each other's back."

* * *

The next day Robert was sitting in the lecture hall waiting for his calculus class to start when he felt someone hovering over him.

"You didn't show for our study group meeting last night," Vanessa said.

"Oh, shit. I'm sorry. I completely forgot about it."

"Look, if you're not going to come to the meetings, then we'll have to find someone else who can help us," Vanessa said as she sat down beside him.

"I'm really sorry," Robert said again. "We had sort of a family crisis at home and my brother and I didn't get back to Waterloo until late last night."

Vanessa studied him, trying to determine if she should believe him or not. "I even started reading up about your nerdy *Magic* game."

Robert had not only missed the study group meeting, but he had also forgotten that he had promised to take her to their *Magic* card game gathering after the study group.

"I'm sorry," Robert said. "Did you really read up on how to play?" Now he felt really guilty.

Before Vanessa had a chance to answer, the professor walked into the lecture hall, threw his briefcase on the desk, and immediately started writing on one of the many whiteboards at the front of the hall. "Okay, pay attention, because I'm only going to go through this once."

There was a collective groan from the class as they all started copying down everything the professor wrote. He was one of the top mathematicians in the world, but it was apparent he could barely tolerate spoon-feeding second year calculus to lesser minds. The students actually preferred when he delegated his teaching duties to one of his assistants.

"You're going to have to explain this to me at next week's study group," Vanessa said as she gathered her books together after the lecture. "I was just copying down everything he wrote, but I didn't understand any of it."

Even Robert was having trouble keeping up with the professor's spew of knowledge. "I'll do my best."

"So, is everything okay with your family?" Vanessa asked as they walked out of the lecture hall.

"Yeah – although for a while there it looked like my brother was going to get arrested."

Vanessa looked confused, but then she pieced what he

said together with the articles that had appeared in the newspaper over the last few days. "That's your brother?"

"Yep, pride of the family."

"Did he really steal data from the U.S. government?"

"No, he didn't steal anything. He just downloaded some stuff they accidently released. They're threatening to arrest anyone who did unless they give it back."

"Does he still have it?"

"No. They took his computer." Robert could tell Vanessa was fascinated by his brother's situation. "You know, they searched *my* computer too."

Vanessa continued to focus on David. "Does he know what was in the data?"

"He says he doesn't." Robert sighed. "I'm heading back to residence. Which way you headed?"

"Same direction – I'll walk with you."

However, when they opened the door to head outside, they discovered it was raining quite heavily.

"Let's take the overpass," Robert suggested.

As they walked through the glass-covered overpass from the Math & Computer building to the Quantum-Nano Centre, they could see the students down below racing to get out of the rain. As they approached the stairwell in the QNC building, Robert was surprised to run into David.

"What are you doing in this building?"

"I went to see one of the professors, but he wasn't in his office."

Vanessa nudged Robert.

"Oh, sorry," Robert said. "David, this is Vanessa. We're in the same calculus class. Vanessa, this is my brother, David."

"Oh, so you're the famous brother that I've been reading about in the newspaper."

"Don't believe everything you read," David said. "I

think they just blew it all out of proportion."

"You heading home?" Robert asked his brother.

"No, I'm actually headed in the other direction. Nice to meet you," he said to Vanessa as he started to walk away.

"Likewise," Vanessa said. "Your brother seems to lead a very exciting life," she said to Robert.

"Not really. I'm sure it'll all die down in a week or so and then he'll be back to his normal boring self."

*** CHAPTER 17 ***

Lou punched the intercom button on his phone and yelled for Laura to come to his office. The last thing he wanted was for this story to die down. Their readership was up since they published the stories about David's arrest, the misidentification of the rifle used by Oswald, and the discrediting of witness statements saying that they'd heard gunshots come from the grassy knoll.

"What have you got?" he asked as Laura entered his office.

"Not much, but I'm still digging." The look on Lou's face told her that was the wrong answer. She decided to throw him a bone to prevent him from chewing her head off. "I may have something about the autopsy."

"Like what?"

"There are numerous records from doctors and nurses at Parkland Memorial Hospital who said that a major portion of the back of the President's head was blown out when he arrived at the hospital. There's also a statement from Roy Kellerman saying that there was a five inch hole in the back of the President's head, suggesting that the shot had come from the front."

"Who's Roy Kellerman?"

"He's the Secret Service agent who was seated next to the driver in the limousine. There's another one from Clint Hill – he's the agent that sheltered the President's body on the way to the hospital – saying that the right rear portion of his head was missing."

"Didn't we already know that?"

"Yeah, but the official autopsy photos and records indicate that the exit wound was on the front of the President's head."

"That doesn't make sense," Lou said.

"There's a bunch more evidence indicating that the autopsy records were falsified. In fact, there's a statement from Douglas Horne – he's the chief analyst with the ARRB – he's 90 to 95% certain that the official autopsy photographs in the National Archives are not of the President's brain."

"Okay, write it up. We'll run it in tomorrow's paper. But we need more. Have you got anything else from your inside source?"

"No," Laura said, "but I'm planning to contact him again later today."

* * *

Laura had told the truth when she said she was planning to meet with her inside source, but she neglected to mention that the meeting had nothing to do with the story. She was leaning up against one of the numerous concrete flower stands outside of the Tribune Tower waiting for Todd to arrive, trying to figure out exactly what she was going to say when he got there. She saw him approach before she had figured it out.

"I brought you a coffee," he said as he handed it to her.

"Thanks," Laura said. She wasn't sure how to start this conversation, but it was apparent she wasn't about to deliver good news.

"I thought we agreed it would be best if we didn't meet in public," Todd said, "so I'm assuming this is really important."

"Yeah, about that," Laura said. "I don't think we should meet anymore at all."

Todd studied her expression. "Yeah, there were a few people at the bureau who wondered whether David had actually turned himself in voluntarily. We're going to have to be more careful."

"That's not what I'm talking about." Laura swirled the coffee around in her cup. "Henry seems to think that we're…involved. I told him that we're just working on a story together, but I don't think he believes me." She took another sip of her coffee. "That's all we're doing here, aren't we?"

Todd didn't answer.

Laura waited for him to look at her. "Sam seems to think that you still have feelings for me. Is she right?"

The expression on Todd's face told her she was. He avoided her gaze and looked up at the building. "I'll do whatever you want me to do."

"I'm sorry," Laura said, reaching over to touch his hand, "but I really want things to work out with Henry."

Todd squeezed her hand, but then let it go. "The timing is actually pretty good," he said matter-of-factly. "The director has been telling me to use up some of my accumulated overtime, so I'm going to be heading out of town for the next few weeks. Got some loose ends to tie up. Take care of yourself."

Todd quickly walked away as if he was late for a very important meeting. He didn't look back.

* * *

The following morning Henry was working in the small meeting room in the Chicago office, the same room he always reserved for his trips there. Sharon, the local systems manager gently tapped on the door. "I was just walking by reception and they said to let you know there's a woman waiting there to see you."

"Did they say who it was?"

"No, but a couple of the associates were tripping over each other trying to chat her up, so you should probably head out there sooner rather than later."

Henry had a feeling he knew who it was. He had been avoiding her calls for over a week now. When he opened the glass doors to the reception area, he was caught by surprise.

"Sam, what are you doing here? Is everything okay?"

"No. Is there somewhere we can talk?"

"Sure." He led her back to the small meeting room. "Can I get you anything?"

"No, I'm fine," Sam said as she sat down.

Henry closed the door to give them some privacy. "What's going on?"

Sam was always one to speak her mind and this was no exception. "I want to know why you're being such an ass." She didn't give Henry time to answer before she continued the assault. "Laura said she's tried to call you a hundred times and you won't take her calls. She didn't do anything wrong, you know. Everything she did was in David's best interest."

"Yeah, I know," Henry said weakly. "I was just a little upset about how close she seems to be with Todd."

"I can assure you there's nothing going on between them. So, unless you want to lose her forever, you better get your shit together and fix this."

Henry knew he had to resolve this one way or another, but he had been afraid. What if his worst fears were true? What if she really did want to go back to Todd?

"I'll call her," Henry said. "I promise."

"Good," Sam said as she rose from her chair. "I'm glad we had this little talk." She opened the door, but paused before leaving. "If you hurt her, I'll be back."

Henry had no intention of hurting her. He picked up the phone and called Laura's number, but it went straight to voice-mail. "I'm sorry," he said. "I'm so, so, sorry. Call me back."

* * *

Laura was in another meeting with her editor. "Okay, this story is starting to gain some traction," Lou said, "but we've got to keep it going. What else you got?"

"There's always been some question as to whether Oswald could have fired three shots so quickly and so accurately," Laura said. "They've done tests with an army specialist who did duplicate the feat, but now there's reports questioning whether Oswald was that good of a shot."

"What do you mean?"

"Oswald's military records indicate he was qualified as a sharpshooter, but in May 1959 he only scored 191 on his test, barely enough to be classified as a marksman, the lowest level of a skilled shooter."

"Yeah, I've always been skeptical," Lou said.

"There are numerous statements that Oswald was working for the CIA for years before the assassination. There's also a report that he met with the FBI two weeks before the assassination and delivered a note to Special Agent James Hosty, although no one knows what was in the note."

"Oswald claimed he was just a patsy in the whole thing," Lou said. "Maybe he was right."

"It sure seems suspicious. And Jack Ruby killed him before he could say anything more."

Lou remembered watching Jack Ruby shoot Oswald on live TV. "It always seemed strange to me how Ruby could get within a few feet of Oswald with a loaded gun when the place was crawling with cops and FBI agents. How could they let that happen?"

"Maybe it was all part of the plan," Laura said.

"Okay. Write it up. We'll run it in tomorrow's paper."

Laura headed back to her desk and saw the message light flashing on her phone. It was almost always flashing. She quickly started flipping through the dozen messages waiting for her, only listening to the first few seconds of each message before moving on to the next. Henry's message was fifth in the queue. She didn't listen to any of the rest.

* * *

"I'm really sorry," Henry said when he answered the phone. "I don't know why I'm so jealous of Todd." That was a lie. Even he wondered why Laura would choose him over Todd. Todd was like the all-star quarterback and he was like the nerdy water-boy. "I'm sorry that I've been such – such an ass – over this whole thing."

"Sam spoke to you, didn't she?"

"Yeah, she came to the office."

"I asked her to stay out of it," Laura said, "but she can be a bit protective of me."

"It was probably something I needed to hear. I'm only in Chicago for today and tomorrow. Any chance I could come over after work today?"

"I would love that. Maybe I'll even cook something. How about six or six-thirty?"

"Sounds perfect."

* * *

Laura could not hide the smile on her face as she hung up the phone. She decided she should listen to the rest of her voice-mail messages before diving into her story again. The last message was from Todd.

"I'm sorry," he said. It was followed by several seconds of dead air with only the background noises of the city coming through. "I was hoping to be able to say goodbye before I left."

Again, there were several seconds of background noise.

"I'm going away for a while and I'm not sure when I'm going to be back. Maybe a week – maybe longer."

There was another pause.

"Maybe forever."

* * *

Henry stopped at a flower shop on his way to Laura's condo. "Do you have any daisies?" he asked the lady at the counter.

"Ooh, I'm not sure. We got some in earlier in the week, but they might all be gone. I'll have to check to see if we've got any more in the back. What's the occasion?"

"No occasion – just trying to apologize for screwing up."

The lady stopped in her tracks. She was an older lady who felt it was her duty to advise her clients on the right flower for any type of occasion. "Are you sure roses wouldn't be a better choice?"

Henry thought back to the first time he had brought Laura flowers. He had chosen daisies because they somehow seemed more cheerful than roses and Laura had loved them. "No, I'd prefer daisies if you've got 'em.

They're sort of our thing."

"Sounds like you know what you're doing," she said with a smile. He heard her rummaging around in the cold room in the back. "You're in luck," she said a few minutes later.

As Henry rode up the elevator in Laura's building, he continued to fuss trying to get the flowers to look just right. He slowly walked down the hall and paused at the door to her unit, trying to figure out what he was going to say first when she opened the door.

Suddenly he heard the elevator ping again and he looked back to see Laura come racing out. "Henry," she said when she saw him. She was carrying two large white bags that smelled delicious. "So much for my plan to cook something for you. I was running late so I decided to just pick up supper at that Peking Duck place down the street. I hope that's okay."

She handed Henry the bags as she fumbled to find her keys to open the door. When they were inside, Henry put the bags on the kitchen counter. "These are for you," he said as he held out the flowers.

Laura took them in her right hand. "Thanks," she said as she gave him a hug. When she kissed him, Henry pulled her in tight. Suddenly the flowers hit the floor and clothes started flying off in every direction.

Supper could wait.

* * *

"This actually tastes pretty good cold," Laura said as she came walking back into the bedroom. She pulled off a piece of the duck and fed it to Henry. They continued to nibble on the duck, and each other, for the next few hours.

"I'm sorry for thinking there was something going on between you and Todd," Henry said. "I should have known I could trust you."

"Yeah, about that," Laura said as she sat up. "It turns out you weren't totally wrong."

Henry sat up, confused.

"Not from my side, but it turns out that Todd may have been looking for something more. I didn't even see it myself until Sam pointed it out."

Henry turned and started to get out of bed.

"But I set him straight," Laura said as she reached out to hold him. "I told him that I'm totally committed and in love with you."

"I knew he had some kind of agenda going on. So you're not going to have anything more to do with him? No more working together? No more – anything?"

"No, I promise."

She pulled Henry back into bed and just lay in his arms. "I'm sorry I didn't see it sooner."

As she lay there, she couldn't help but think about the voice-mail Todd had left her. He said he was going away for a while – maybe forever. What was he going to do?

*** CHAPTER 18 ***

David slowly walked out of University Stadium after their early morning soccer practice. The coach had worked the team particularly hard that morning, not because they'd lost their game against York, but because they'd sagged in the second half after building up a two-nil lead in the first. York had scored a goal late in the game and almost got the equalizer in injury time. To say the coach was a little pissed would be an understatement.

Since David's residence was only a few blocks from the stadium, he had decided to walk to practice that morning, something that his aching muscles now regretted. As he turned onto Seagram Drive, he noticed a black Town Car idling along the side of the road. The tinted windows hid who was inside.

David briefly considered crossing to the other side of the street so he wouldn't have to walk by the car, but then convinced himself that he was just being paranoid. As he approached the car, the window on the passenger side hummed as it slowly lowered.

"Can I give you a lift?" the man inside asked.

David crouched down so he could see who was asking the question. The man looked to be about sixty years old and was very well dressed. Since he had only met him once, it took David a few seconds to recognize that it was Simon Westbrook, the head of the secret society.

"Mr. Westbrook. What can I do for you?"

"Get in, get in," Mr. Westbrook said as he waved for David to get into the car. "It's best if we talk in private."

David took a quick look around to see if anyone else was watching, but the only people he saw were a few of his teammates walking in the other direction. He opened the car door and climbed in.

"I hear things have been pretty exciting for you of late," Mr. Westbrook said as he slowly pulled away from the curb.

"Scary would be a better word," David said.

Mr. Westbrook took a quick glance at David. "I'm sure it was."

Mr. Westbrook made several unnecessary turns, continually checking his rearview mirror to make sure they weren't being followed. David was surprised when he turned off Westmount Drive and down a small deserted road that led to the Environmental Reserve. He pulled off to the side of the road.

"I'm sorry, but I haven't been able to pick up any messages because the cops took my laptop," David said. "I had to give it to them or else they would have put me in jail."

"Don't worry about that. They won't find anything on the laptop. We'll get you another one, but it's probably best if you keep a low profile for the time being. They're watching you, you know."

David did have an eerie feeling that he was being watched. This just confirmed it.

"We know that the packages you distributed were all

received," Mr. Westbrook said. "All except one. Do you still have the seventh package?"

"No, I was never told who to deliver it to, so I just hid it. The police were after me. I didn't know what else to do."

"You did the right thing."

"Should I go get it and bring it to you?"

"No, you've already done enough. Is it safe where it is?"

"I think so."

"Anyone else know where it is?"

"Yeah, but I think we can trust him. He hid me from the police when they were chasing me."

Mr. Westbrook looked concerned. "What's his name?"

"Nigel Livingston. He's a professor in the Quantum-Nano Centre on the Waterloo campus. He taped the microchip to the back of the picture of his wife on his desk. He said he'd keep it safe."

"How are you supposed to get it back from him?"

"He said I could just come to his office whenever I wanted it back. I tried, but he wasn't there. Should I contact him?"

"No, that would be too dangerous," Mr. Westbrook said. "Remember, they're watching you. I'll make arrangements to get it back."

Mr. Westbrook started the car, did a U-turn, and began the drive back to David's residence. However, he stopped the car a few blocks away. "It's probably best if I let you out here. Just keep a low profile until we let you know it's safe."

David got out of the car and watched him drive away. When he turned around to walk back to his residence, he was surprised to see Bronx standing in front of him.

"Who was that?" she asked.

"Just a friend who gave me a lift."

"Must be nice to have friends who drive expensive cars

like that. You'll have to introduce me."

"I don't think he's your type." David took a quick look around to see if anyone else was watching him. "What are you doing here?"

"Just walkin' back to residence. You seem a little spooked. Are you gettin' yourself into trouble again?"

"Trouble? What makes you think I'm getting myself into trouble?"

"You seem to have a knack for finding it. Remember, I can't really watch your back if you won't tell me what's goin' on."

* * *

Professor Nigel Livingston stared at the picture of his wife on his desk. It was late on a Friday night and his wife had abandoned him for a "ladies weekend" retreat with her friends, leaving him wondering what he was going to do with himself for the next few days.

He flipped the picture around to see the microchip still securely taped to the back of the picture. He had been fighting his curiosity for weeks now. He really didn't care what was on the microchip, but because he had been told that it was encrypted, it was like a temptress who continued to taunt and tease him. He had never encountered an encryption he couldn't crack.

Finally, he couldn't stand it anymore and he carefully pulled the tape away and loaded the microchip into an external black box that had adapters for every type of memory device known to man. He could see there were two files on the microchip, a large file that presumably contained the data, and the second, a small file that presumably held the key to unlocking the contents. He copied both files to his computer so he could begin his analysis. Then he re-taped the microchip onto the back of the picture.

After several hours of work, he still hadn't cracked the encryption. Everything he tried, failed. Whoever had created this encryption was good, very good. He was missing something. One key to unlocking the content was readily apparent and he had found that within the first hour of his attempt. However, the second key, and he was sure this was a two-key encryption, continued to elude him.

He glanced at his watch and saw that it was three-thirty in the morning and decided it was time to head home. He would tackle it again tomorrow.

* * *

Professor Livingston was sound asleep when he suddenly opened his eyes and bolted straight up in bed.

"I know what the second key is," he shouted. Fortunately, he wife wasn't there to hear his exclamation for it surely would have scared her to death, or at least convinced her that he had finally lost his mind. "The second key is the device itself," he said to himself. "Brilliant. Every time the data is copied, it uses something on the device itself as a second encryption key. That way, if someone intercepts the data during transmission, they won't be able to read it unless they have the actual device it was created for. Every copy is different!"

The clock radio beside his bed showed that it was just after six in the morning, but he had to find out right away if his theory was correct. To do that, he would have to use the microchip that David had given him, not the copy he had put on his computer. He threw on his clothes and raced back to the university.

He unlocked his office door, raced over to his desk, picked up the picture of his wife and turned it around.

The microchip was gone.

* * *

David was still half asleep when his phone rang. Whoever was calling had called his residence phone rather than his cell phone. That confused him, as all of his friends and family normally called or texted his cell. "Hello," he said after stumbling out of bed.

"It's gone," the person on the phone said. He hadn't identified himself, but David knew who it was. "Did you take it?" the professor asked.

"No, but I think I know who did," David answered. He was quite sure Simon Westbrook was the one who had arranged to retrieve the microchip.

"I was expecting you to contact me by now to get it, but I got worried when it suddenly disappeared."

"I'm sure everything is okay," David reassured him. "You shouldn't have called me on this phone. They may be listening."

David was right. Someone was listening.

* * *

After he hung up the phone, the professor was frustrated, not because he cared what was on the microchip, but because he wouldn't be able to prove his theory about how to break the encryption. Or maybe he would. He still had a copy of the files on his computer, but if his theory was correct, it would use a different encryption key.

"Every copy is encrypted using a different second key," he mumbled to himself. "Something unique to the particular device." He was determined to solve the puzzle.

*** CHAPTER 19 ***

"You're life value is down to zero," Robert said to Vanessa. "You're out of the game."

Robert had taken Vanessa to one of their *Magic* games after their study session, loaned her a set of cards so she could play, and was trying to teach her the complicated strategy involved to be successful.

"Shit – shit – shit," she said. "I thought for sure I was going to win. What did I do wrong?"

She was much more into the game than Robert expected. "You were too aggressive," he said.

"But isn't the point of the game to destroy your opponent?"

"Yes, but you also have to maintain a balance or else your opponent will destroy you."

Vanessa was still excited from the game. "Kill, or be killed is my motto." She reached out and touched Robert's arm. "This is a really cool game. Thanks for taking me."

They continued to talk about strategy as they walked through the deserted campus after the game had finished.

Robert didn't want their night to end just yet. "Want to

go for coffee?"

"Sure."

They found a table in a small café just off campus and spent the next hour giving each other their life histories. Vanessa reached out to touch his hand when he told her about his mother's battle with cancer, which she lost when he was seventeen.

"That must have been rough," she said.

"It threw me for a while, but I think it hurt my dad and my brother even more. I hated going home because it felt like a funeral parlour. We used to whisper to each other when we were there – not sure why. But it got better after we moved to a new house and my Grandma came to live with us. She's the one who pushed us to get on with our lives. Said we had to do something to make our Mom proud."

Robert could feel his eyes start to water. "What about your parents?"

"I never really knew them. They died in a car accident when I was a baby. I was raised by my aunt and uncle."

Robert felt the trembling in her hand. "I'm so sorry. Do you have any brothers or sisters?"

"No, just me."

Vanessa pulled her hand away as she suddenly sat straight up in her chair. "*No time to feel sorry for yourself* my uncle used to say. He was in the military." She lowered her voice as if she was imitating him. "A good soldier doesn't cry. There's work to be done here. Back to your post."

Vanessa looked a little embarrassed. She avoided looking at Robert and looked around the café. "Isn't that your brother sitting over there?"

Robert looked over his shoulder. He hadn't seen David when they first arrived at the café and he had been so engrossed in their conversation since then, he hadn't noticed much else.

"Yep, that's him. I didn't see him come in."

"Should we go over and join him?"

Robert was getting increasingly annoyed over how everyone seemed to be fascinated with his brother these days. "No, he looks like he's meeting with one of his professors." He tried to re-engage Vanessa in their conversation, but he could see that she continually glanced over at his brother.

"The professor just left," Vanessa said a few minutes later. "Should we ask him to join us now?"

"Whoa, is that his girlfriend?" Vanessa said before Robert had a chance to answer.

Robert looked over his shoulder and saw that Bronx was sitting at the chair vacated by the professor. She was leaning in so there wasn't much space between them.

"No, my brother's got a girlfriend back in our hometown – and that ain't her."

Vanessa raised an eyebrow.

"We should probably go," Robert said. "I've got a class first thing in the morning."

When they got up to leave, David noticed them and immediately increased the space between him and Bronx to a more respectable distance. "Hey," David said as they walked by. "Sorry, I didn't see you in here."

"Obviously," Robert said. "I'll see you back at the residence."

* * *

"Things looked pretty cozy back there at the café," Robert said when David came through the door of their suite back at the residence.

"We're just friends," David said. "There's nothing going on between us."

"Really? All evidence to the contrary."

"Really," David said. "I've told Bronx a million times that I've already got a girlfriend."

"Well, you're not acting like you do. I just hope you know what you're doing."

David hated how Robert seemed to act more like his father than his brother now that they were away from home. He was old enough to live his own life and make his own decisions. "Just stay out of it." He headed into his bedroom, slamming the door shut behind him.

It was about five minutes later when David opened the door again and came back into the small living room. He threw himself onto the chair.

"I don't know what to do," he said to Robert. "Ashley is a great girlfriend. She's smart, she's good-looking. I feel really comfortable when I'm with her. She's perfect in every way."

"I feel a *but* coming," Robert said.

David buried his head in his hands. "But Bronx excites me. I don't really know much about her at all. She's pushy as hell – at times, she can be a real pain in the ass – but…"

Robert knew his brother was not the type of person to string two girls along. "I think you know what you have to do."

"Really? Cause I have no clue."

"It's easy," Robert said. "All you have to do is decide."

"Easier said, than done."

* * *

David tossed and turned all night as he struggled with his decision. He bolted awake just after seven – with a plan. It was obvious what he had to do. It seemed so logical and simple. He'd known Ashley for years – knew everything about her. But he didn't know much about Bronx at all.

Maybe that's why he was fascinated with her. He would simply get to know Bronx a little better. Then he'd have all of the facts – the pros and cons of each of them. A simple apples-to-apples comparison would make the decision easy. He had a plan.

"Meet for lunch at the café?" he texted Bronx.

"Sure," came the response a few seconds later. "Have class until 11:30. 11:45?"

"OK," David texted back.

He arrived about fifteen minutes early, a rarity for him, and found a small table-for-two tucked into the corner of the café. He threw his backpack onto the seat to hold the table and then went to the counter to order a sandwich and a smoothie. When he sat down, he made sure he'd be able to see Bronx as soon as she came through the door.

She arrived a few minutes late, but that was no big deal to David. He was notoriously late most times himself, something that always seemed to annoy Ashley. Advantage – Bronx.

He waved to Bronx, who waved back. She signaled that she was going to grab something at the counter before coming over to join him. When she did, David noticed she had chosen the same smoothie as he had. Ashley didn't like them – said they were filled with sugar. Bronx – two. Ashley – nothing.

"I was surprised to get your text," Bronx said as she sat down. "What's the occasion?"

"Nothing. I just thought it would be nice if we got together for lunch."

Bronx was wearing her blue "*I Love New York*" T-shirt, David's favourite. "What made you choose Laurier over a U.S. school?" he asked. "New York has some pretty good universities."

"Cause of my parents – They're splittin' up and I wanted

to be closer to Mom. She was born in Canada and decided to move back when things started to fall apart. She's got a place just north of Toronto, so I try to see her every few weeks."

"Sorry to hear about your parents. Are you close to your dad?"

"Used to be, but my dad's a cop so he can be a bit strict. We've butted heads more and more over the last few years." She took a long sip from her smoothie. "People say I get my aggressiveness from my dad."

David thought for a minute as he took a bite of his sandwich. Bronx was definitely aggressive. Ashley was the exact opposite. David felt totally relaxed and at ease when he was with her.

"So are you going to stay in Canada after you get your degree?" David asked.

"Hell, no. I'm goin' back to New Yawk for sure. I'm just up here for a few years to support my mom."

Point lost for Bronx. David had no desire to live in the U.S., and in particular, New York.

"What would you do in New York?" he asked.

"Dunno. One of the nice things about New Yawk is you can do pretty much anythin' you want. If they don't got it there, it prob'ly don't exist."

"I mean, what kind of career do you see for yourself?"

"You mean, what do I wanna be when I grow up?"

"Yeah, I guess so," David said.

Bronx stopped eating and studied David. "What's goin' on?"

"What do you mean?"

"Suddenly I feel like I'm on a job interview."

David could feel his face start to flush. "I'm just trying to get to know you better so I know if we – I mean, if there's any chance that we…" He had no idea how to finish the sentence.

"This is like your stupid roommate questionnaire all over again," she said. "You don't decide to be with someone based on which box they tick on a survey."

She quickly reached down to pick up her backpack. "Goodbye," she said as she stood up. "I hope you find someone who scores better than I do on yer stupid test."

She stormed from the café before David could stop her. This was not part of his plan. It was a stupid plan.

*** CHAPTER 20 ***

"Laura – my office," Lou bellowed. There was no need for him to use the intercom as his voice seemed to carry the entire length of the office anyway. "I've been thinking," he said when Laura entered his office.

"Uh, oh," Laura thought to herself. It was never a good thing when her boss got to thinking.

"I've been thinking that your series of stories has done a pretty good job of convincing people that Oswald didn't act alone and that there was some kind of conspiracy, but now we need to move forward and say exactly who was involved."

"I'm not sure I have enough evidence yet to do that."

"Okay, walk me through what you've got so far."

"Well, for starters, there's some evidence to suggest the CIA may have been involved."

"Like what?"

"The CIA has repeatedly said that Oswald wasn't connected to them, but there's growing evidence that he was. There are reports that both the CIA and FBI were alerted that Oswald was a potential threat to the President in Dallas and that they withheld this information – some say deliberately."

"Why would the CIA want Kennedy dead?"

"There's speculation that they weren't happy that both the President and his brother, Bobby, were trying to appease their relationship with Cuba and the Soviet Union. The President was apparently in the process of putting the CIA on a short leash after the Bay of Pigs fiasco."

"But the President signed off on that," Lou said.

"Yes, but it was a CIA-led operation that failed miserably and there are reports that they withheld critical information from the President."

"I find it hard to believe that the CIA would be involved in a plot to assassinate their own President," Lou said. "We can't run a story without some real evidence. We're not the National Enquirer, you know. What else you got?"

"There's speculation that the Mafia may have been involved."

"Come on," Lou said. "The Mafia is not sophisticated enough to take on the assassination of the President."

"Actually, some members of the Mafia were experts in assassinations. They were trained by the CIA and worked with them in several attempts to take out Castro."

"Castro? Why would the Mafia want to kill Castro?"

"Because the Mafia used to control all of the casinos in Cuba. All of that changed in the Cuban Revolution when Castro gained power. The CIA, the Mafia and anti-Castro Cubans were all in bed together – had been for several years."

Lou was still having trouble getting his head around this theory.

"And there's a ton of evidence connecting Jack Ruby to the Mob," Laura added.

"I still find it hard to believe."

"There's also a theory that the defense companies may have wanted Kennedy taken out," Laura said. "When President Eisenhower left office, he warned the nation about the power of the military establishment and the arms industry. There was talk that Kennedy planned to end the involvement of the U.S. in Vietnam, and that's not what the defense contractors wanted."

"It sounds like there was no shortage of people who wanted the President dead. Is there any new evidence indicating who was actually involved?"

"Not that I've found so far."

"What about those eleven hundred documents that disappeared? Have you found any of those yet?"

"Not yet," Laura said. "If anyone's still got them, they're not talking."

"We can't run a story suggesting who's behind the conspiracy with what you've got so far. We need more. Can your inside source get us anything?"

"I don't think so." Laura put her head down. "I seem to have lost communication with him."

"Well I suggest you regain communication with him – and fast. And find me those missing documents!"

* * *

"What is your citizenship and place of birth?" the Canadian customs agent asked Todd as he crossed the border.

"American," Todd said. "I was born in Chicago."

The customs agent looked at Todd. "Please remove your sunglasses." He compared his face to the one on his passport. Then he scanned the bar-code on the passport into his computer and watched as the terminal displayed the results.

"What is the purpose of your trip to Canada?"

"Hunting – I'm heading to a hunting lodge up north to do some moose hunting."

The customs agent took a closer look at Todd. "Are you bringing any firearms with you across the border?"

"Yes," Todd said as he picked up a piece of paper that was sitting on the passenger seat of the car. "Here's my permit." He handed the agent the permit.

"This is not the normal type of gun used for hunting moose," the agent said as he studied the *Authorization to Transport* form.

"Yeah, it's my first time hunting moose so I wasn't sure exactly what to bring. I've also got a *Temporary Firearms Borrowing License*. The lodge said they could loan me a rifle if I needed it." Todd handed him the second form.

"Exactly where is this hunting lodge?"

"Somewhere north of Sault St. Marie," Todd said. He handed him a pamphlet. "The exact address is written on the back. I hope I don't get lost trying to find it."

The customs agent studied the pamphlet and forms carefully. "Could I ask you to step out of the vehicle and open your trunk sir?"

Todd pulled the latch to release the trunk. As he got out of the vehicle, he became aware that a second customs agent was now watching his every move.

The first customs agent lifted a suitcase which revealed the heavy steel case that contained the rifle. "Is that case locked?"

"Yes it is," Todd said. "I'm with the FBI, so I know how to properly secure firearms while they're being transported." Todd showed him his FBI identification. "Would you like me to open it?"

The customs agent visibly relaxed when he realized he was dealing with an FBI agent. "Not here. Just pull off to the side, go inside the building, and one of our agents will come out to verify that the serial number on the gun matches the permit. You should have let me know earlier you're an FBI agent. We immediately go on alert whenever we become aware of firearms – can never be too careful these days."

"I'm sure," Todd said. "Sorry, but I'm just here on vacation, not official business, so I didn't want to play the FBI card."

Todd got back into his car and followed the directions of the second customs agent who pointed out where he should park.

"Okay, I'll get you to unlock the gun case now so I can verify the serial number," he said. The customs agent barely glanced at the rifle before he put his initials in the box on the form. "Just take this inside and they should have you on your way in no time at all. Good luck hunting."

"Thanks," Todd said as he locked the gun case.

Less than twenty minutes later, Todd was on the highway heading out of Sault Ste. Marie. As he approached a major intersection, he read the signs providing directions as to which way to go. One road headed north toward the hunting lodge; the other road headed south toward Waterloo. He turned south.

* * *

Professor Nigel Livingston continued his work in his office on the Waterloo campus. He was not going to quit until he knew if his encryption theory was correct. It would have been a lot easier if he still had the microchip, but that was an obstacle he would have to overcome. He still had the encrypted files on his computer, and he was sure he had one of the encryption keys. If his theory was correct, the second key would be hardware based.

Many people know that computers communicate over the Internet using their IP address, but he had to go much deeper than that. As his computer started up, he entered the key sequence to interrupt the process so he could see the Media Access Control address of each component of his computer. He wrote down the MAC-48 address of his disk controller, but he suspected he would have to go even deeper. He also wrote down the burned in address of the disk itself.

As an encryption specialist, the professor knew the capabilities available to those who tracked all of this type of information. There were rumours that the U.S. National Security Agency had a system that could monitor the movements of everyone in a city by monitoring the MAC addresses of their devices, whether it was their cell phone or a chip in their car. Some manufacturers had even stopped using burned in addresses for devices to prevent *Big Brother* from watching.

The professor made another copy of the encrypted files onto an external drive. If his theory was correct, the files would be encrypted using a hardware identifier from the external drive. He wrote down the hardware address of that device.

He planned to use a brute-force attack to break the encryption using the two copies of the files as test subjects. He knew such an attack could take hours, maybe even days or weeks. Fortunately, the professor had access to some of the most powerful computers available at the university.

He entered the required information into the system and hit the key to start the code-breaking program.

Now all he had to do was wait.

*** CHAPTER 21 ***

David threw himself onto his bed when he got back to his room after his lunch with Bronx. Things had not gone at all how he had planned and he was pretty sure Bronx would never speak to him again. He decided to skip his afternoon classes and just sleep away the afternoon.

He awoke a few hours later when his cell phone chirped the arrival of a new text message.

"Planning to come to Waterloo 2nite," the message said. "R U around?"

The text was from Ashley and couldn't have come at a better time for David.

"Yes," he texted back. "How R U getting here?"

"My parents. 7 OK?"

"Perfect"

David was filled with energy again. Ashley was the perfect girl for him. No doubt about it. He wondered why he had ever doubted it in the first place.

David heard Robert come through the door into their suite. "Ashley's coming over tonight."

"You're not going to break up with her here, are you?"

Robert asked.

"I'm not breaking up with her. Why would you think that?"

"What about Bronx?"

"It's over with her," David said. "Actually, it never really got started. We're not compatible." He didn't want to share any of the details of their lunch.

Robert looked completely confused.

"But don't say anything about Bronx when Ashely's here," David said. "Okay?"

"Okay," Robert said. He was still confused.

* * *

It was a few hours later when David received a text message from Ashley saying they were just pulling into the parking lot of his building. David raced from his room and hit the button for the elevator, but grew impatient so he decided to take the stairs. He reached the lobby just in time to see Ashley and her parents approaching the main doors.

"Hi Ashley," David said as he held the outside door open. He wanted to give her a hug, but felt awkward with her parents watching. "Hello, Mr. and Mrs. Taylor."

"Hi David," Mr. Taylor said. "How are your classes going so far?"

"Pretty good."

Mrs. Taylor pulled her daughter in close. "Just call us when you're ready," she whispered. "We'll only be a few minutes away."

Mrs. Taylor gave David a weak smile. "We should go," she said to her husband.

"Why don't you show me your residence?" Ashley asked David.

"There's not much to show," he said as he took her hand and led her into the building. He pointed out the cafeteria as they walked by it on their way to the elevators. "Meals here are optional, but most students sign up for at least one meal a day. Robert and I are registered for both breakfast and supper, but we normally just grab lunch somewhere on campus."

There were only a few students sitting in the cafeteria as most had already finished supper.

"Can we just go to your room?" Ashley asked.

"You read my mind," David said suggestively. He quickly pushed the button for the elevator. "We're in W308. Robert's there, but I'm sure I can get rid of him."

As soon as they were in the elevator, David pulled her in close. She hugged him back, but David had a sense that she was nervous.

"This is it," David said as he opened the door to W308. "It's not much, but its home. The common area is a bit small, but it's big enough. Dad let us bring a TV and a loveseat from home – the chairs they supplied are as hard as rock – and it's got a sink and small fridge. Can I get you anything?"

"No, I'm good," Ashley said.

"My room's off to the right," David said as he pointed to it, "and this is Robert's room to the left. All the bedrooms in the building are identical – just mirror images of each other."

Robert was sitting at his desk doing something on his computer, but looked up when they poked their heads in. "Hi Ashley. Good to see you."

"Hi Robert."

"Don't you have a class tonight?" David asked his brother. David already knew that he didn't, but hoped he'd pick up that he wanted to be alone with Ashley.

"Vanessa is supposed to be coming over to study in a few minutes," Robert said, "but we can work in the cafeteria."

As he gathered up his laptop and his books, he couldn't help but notice the worried look on Ashley's face.

* * *

"What are you doing down here?" Vanessa said when she found Robert waiting for her by the elevators on the main floor.

"David's girlfriend is in town and they didn't want me as their chaperone."

"I wonder why?" Vanessa said as she winked. "Do you want to head over to my place to study?"

"No. Let's just hang out in the cafeteria here for a bit. I have a gut feeling that something's not right."

They each grabbed a coffee and sat at a small table. Sure enough, Robert saw Ashley get out of the elevator about ten minutes later. She was crying as she headed out of the main doors and Robert saw her mother waiting for her just outside.

"Sorry, but I think I'm going to have to give you a rain-check on our study session," Robert said. "I'm going to go check on my brother."

"Is there anything I can do to help?"

"I don't think so. I'll just see you at the group study session on Thursday. Are you going to come to our next *Magic* gathering?"

"You can count on it," Vanessa said. She threw her coffee cup in the garbage as she got up to leave. "I hope everything is okay with your brother."

* * *

When Robert entered their room, he found David lying on his bed staring at the ceiling. He looked as white as a ghost.

"Is everything okay?" Robert asked.

David continued to just stare at the ceiling. "Ashley broke up with me," he finally said. "I don't understand. We were perfect for each other."

"Is there anything I can do?"

David still hadn't blinked. "She said she's started seeing someone – someone in her art class."

"I'm sorry," Robert said.

"Did you hear me?" David said as he sat up. "An artist – a fucking artist. He doesn't play any sports – not one!"

Robert put down his backpack and sat down in David's desk chair. This was going to be a long night.

* * *

On the following Thursday, Robert talked his brother into going with them to their *Magic* gathering. He had to do something; David had been moping around for several days.

"Now, remember – try not to be so aggressive," Robert advised Vanessa. He had created a card deck for her that he was sure would help her do better than she had the first time she played.

Vanessa looked through her deck. "I think I need more blue cards." Blue cards were used in the game by players who wanted to use a strategy of trickery and manipulation. She looked at David. "Do you have any blue cards that you're willing to trade?"

David had brought his own deck. He knew the basics of the game, but wasn't into it as much as his brother. "Sure. I'll give you a blue one if you give me a white one." White's values were order, protection, light and law.

"Done," Vanessa said.

"Be careful," Robert advised. "Building a strong deck is pretty hard."

"We're okay," Vanessa said. "I'll trade you another white for one of your black cards," Vanessa said to David. Black was the colour of death, ambition and darkness.

"Don't do it," Robert warned.

"Afraid I'm going to take you down?" Vanessa teased.

"Bring it on," Robert said. "Don't say I didn't warn you."

Less than an hour later, both David and Vanessa had been eliminated from the game. Robert didn't finish first, but he had done a lot better than they did.

"Do you want to get a coffee?" Robert asked them as they were leaving.

"How about the Bombshelter?" Vanessa asked. "I think David here needs something a little stronger."

The Bombshelter was the pub located in the basement of the Student Life Centre. It was appropriately named, but the decor didn't seem to matter to the numerous undergrads who frequented the place.

"I'm up for it," David said.

Robert wasn't that keen, but it was the first sign of life he'd seen out of his brother in days, so he relented.

"Sorry to hear you broke up with your girlfriend," Vanessa said to David when they were at the pub.

"Thanks. I thought we were perfect for each other, but she's started seeing an artist. An artist – can you believe that?"

"What about that girl I saw you with at the café last week? She looked interesting."

"Oh, she's definitely interesting," David said. "But I screwed that one up as well. In case you hadn't noticed, I'm not very good with women."

David was turning this into a pity party. It didn't take him long to knock back several beers.

Vanessa tried to change the subject. "Why don't you

150

tell me what happened to you in Chicago?"

David told her the story about his arrest in Chicago. He also told her how he had snuck across the border. She seemed fascinated with how clever he was.

"Come on, you must have taken a peek at what was in those files," Vanessa said. She had been knocking drinks back at a pretty good pace herself and was beginning to gush over David.

He seemed to be enjoying the attention. "No, the files were encrypted. I don't know what was in them." He leaned over and whispered into Vanessa's ear. "But I think it's something the government is trying to cover-up."

"No shit," Vanessa said. "I'd sure like to see what was in those files. Do you have a copy?"

"I did, but not anymore." David was really starting to slur his words.

"What happened to it?"

"The professor said someone took it."

"What professor?"

"One of the prof's at Waterloo – His email address is *Enigma*." Along with slurring his words, David was getting louder and louder. "*Enigma*. Is that a cool handle, or what?"

"Okay, I think it's time to call it a night," Robert said. He had been sipping the same beer all night and was several drinks behind David and Vanessa. "I think you've both had enough."

Robert had an arm on each of them as he helped them up the stairs out of the pub. He was glad to see a taxi parked outside and helped Vanessa into the back seat.

"Make sure she gets home safely," he said to the driver. He handed him a twenty dollar bill.

"For sure," the driver said. He knew the address that Vanessa had given him was only about a ten dollar fare away.

"And could you call another cab for my brother and I?"

The driver used his radio to call another taxi. "It should be here in less than five."

"You're a good brother," David said after the taxi had left. He leaned in and gave him a hug. "Thanks for taking care of me."

"Someone's got to," Robert said.

* * *

The following morning David was up early because he had soccer practice. The first time he got out of bed, he felt dizzy and he was sure he was going to throw up, but he fought through it. The coach had told all of the players how important it was to attend practices and David wanted to live up to his commitments.

He stepped out of the building and began the walk to the stadium, which was only a few blocks away. The air was crisp this morning, which made him feel a bit better. He'd woken up several times the night before in a hot sweat.

As he walked along the sidewalk, he recognized the big black car parked against the curb. "Can I give you a ride?" Simon Westbrook asked.

"Sure," David said as he climbed into the passenger seat.

"You look like hell," Mr. Westbrook said. "Rough night?"

"It's been rough the whole week."

Mr. Westbrook pulled away from the curb and made several unnecessary turns, checking his rear-view mirror each time to make sure they weren't being followed. He finally pulled into a deserted parking lot in front of a building that had large black letters and numbers etched into the glass.

"Where are we?" David asked.

"This is the Optometry building. One of my best friends went to school here – one of only two such schools in all of Canada."

David looked at the glass entrance again. He subconsciously started reading the letters of varying sizes as if he was reading an eye chart. Except this glass wall had sort of a 3D holographic effect. He suddenly felt nauseous again and had to look away.

"I brought you something," Mr. Westbrook said as he reached into the back seat of the car. He gave David a laptop that looked almost identical to the one that had been confiscated by the U.S. prosecutor. "It should work exactly the same as your old one."

David unzipped his soccer bag, lifted up the panel in the bottom of the bag, and slid the laptop inside.

"We never did find the microchip in the professor's office," Mr. Westbrook said.

David looked alarmed. "The professor said someone removed it from the back of the picture of his wife. I figured it was you. Who else could have taken it?"

"Probably the same people who have been watching you. They're desperate to recover all copies of whatever's in those files."

"I'm sorry," David said. "I guess I shouldn't have hidden it with the professor."

"It's not your fault." Mr. Westbrook started up the car. "We should go – don't want you to be late for practice."

They drove back toward University Stadium, again taking some unnecessary turns to make sure they weren't being followed. Mr. Westbrook stopped the car about a block away from the stadium.

"This will be our last face-to-face meeting," he said as David got out of the car. "I'll send a message to you on your computer if I need you to do anything else. It's probably best to keep a low profile for the time being. And please – please be careful."

* * *

When Professor Livingston arrived at his office that morning, he did what he had done every morning for the last four days – check the status of his code-breaking program. Whoever had designed the encryption algorithm was good, because it normally didn't take this long to crack. However, this morning the terminal displayed the message he was waiting for – *Decryption completed.*

He scanned the list of files displayed on his computer and opened a few of them to make sure the decryption had been successful. Everything looked good. It appeared they were just a series of reports, nothing out of the ordinary as far as he could see.

He picked up his phone to call David, but it went to voice-mail. "Hi, it's Professor Nigel Livingston. I've managed to get a copy of the files you wanted. Give me a call or send me an email if you still want them."

Then he turned his focus to the thing he was really interested in – the encryption algorithm.

It was a few hours later when David called him back, after he had finished soccer practice. "I can't believe you recovered the files."

"I told you there wasn't an encryption that I couldn't crack," the professor bragged. "Do you still want the files or should I just delete them?"

"Sure. Could you burn them to a CD for me?"

"No problem, but it will take several CDs. There's quite a lot of data. Do you want to swing by my office to pick them up when they're ready?"

"No, it's probably better if we meet somewhere else. I'll call you later with a location. I've got classes all day so it probably won't be until this evening."

"Or tomorrow," the professor said. "I'm in no rush."

"We'd better not wait until tomorrow. Somebody pinched these files from your office once already. I'd rather not give them a second chance."

* * *

When he got back to his residence, David pulled the laptop out of his soccer bag and fired it up.

"*May have recovered files,*" he typed into the computer. "*Picking them up later tonight. What should I do with them?*"

It was only a few minutes later when David received a response. "*Too dangerous. You are being watched. Please advise time and location of meeting. Will provide backup.*"

David hadn't set a time or location with the professor yet. Too dangerous? Why would it be dangerous? He was sure he could shake a few cops if they were still tailing him.

He entered his response into the computer. "*Time and location TBD.*"

* * *

Burning all of these files to CDs was taking the professor a lot longer than he expected. 10% completed. 12% completed. And this was just the second CD of about six that would be required. This was going to take forever. He decided to take a look at what was in some of the files while he waited.

The first few files he opened seemed to be just page after page of notes and reports. Boooring.

He opened one of the larger files and saw that it was a video. As soon as he saw it, he knew what it was. It was a video of JFK on that fateful day in 1963, but this wasn't the Zapruder film that the whole world had seen before. This video was shot from an entirely different angle.

The professor watched as the President's motorcade approached. The President was smiling and waving to the crowd, as was Jackie Kennedy. Suddenly everything changed. The President reached up to his throat with both hands. Jackie grabbed his left elbow and seemed to be trying to figure out what the problem was. A split-second later, the President's head exploded. Even though the professor knew what was going to happen, he still felt sick to his stomach when he saw it.

Why hadn't anyone seen this video before?

The professor clicked on the next video file. Once again, this was a video that he'd never seen before. It was shot from the grassy knoll. Like the other one, it showed the President smiling and waving to the crowd. But then it quickly changed, as if whoever was holding the camera had fallen down or dropped the camera. It showed nothing but a close-up of the grass for a few seconds. Then the camera moved again, as whoever was holding the camera tried to pick it up.

That's when the professor saw it – the flash of gunfire from behind the wall.

He had seen the second shooter.

The professor grabbed his phone to call David. "David, please pick up." But his call went to voice-mail again. "David – I looked at the files. I know who the second shooter is."

*** CHAPTER 22 ***

"We can't run this," Lou said when Laura appeared in his doorway at the Chicago Tribune. "This is just hypothesis and speculation. There's no real evidence or facts."

Laura reached out and caught the copy when he threw it in her direction. Although she had been working hard on the story for the last few days, she knew he was right. "I'll keep digging."

When she got back to her desk, she started to call Todd but then hung up before the call went through. She had promised she wouldn't call him anymore, but she was desperate. She needed someone with inside knowledge. This wasn't personal – this was for her story. She dialed the number again.

She was surprised when the call was redirected to the main switchboard. "Federal Bureau of Investigation – How may I direct your call?"

Laura briefly thought about hanging up, but then reconsidered. This was the FBI; they'd be able to figure out who was calling regardless. "I'd like to speak to agent Todd Knight please."

"Just a moment please."

It was almost a minute later when someone came on the line. "This is agent Brian Clark. How may I help you?"

Laura recognized the name as he had been Todd's partner at the bureau for quite a few years. He knew of her past relationship with Todd. "Hi Brian. This is Laura Walsh. I'm trying to get ahold of Todd. Do you have a number where I can reach him?"

"I wish I did. When's the last time you spoke to him?"

"Almost a week ago now. Why?"

"Because he resigned four days ago. We haven't heard from him since."

"Resigned? Are you sure? He said he was going to burn some of his overtime and get away somewhere, but he didn't say anything about resigning."

"Well, something's got him really upset. He was acting really weird."

Laura sighed. "I think I might know what caused it. It might have been me – something I said."

"Well the Director said he'd just hold onto his resignation for a few weeks – not do anything just in case he changed his mind. He's a great agent – the best – took his oath to *defend the Constitution of the United States against all enemies, foreign and domestic* to heart."

Laura knew how seriously Todd took his commitment to his duty. Resigning just didn't make sense.

"Let me know if you hear from him," Laura said, "and I'll do the same."

After she hung up the phone, Laura recalled the last voice-mail that Todd had left her. "I'll be going away for a while – maybe a week – maybe forever." Now she was really worried.

* * *

David had felt his cellphone vibrate in his pocket several times while he was in class so he knew someone was trying to reach him. But he also knew his calculus professor was strictly against anyone using their cellphone during his lectures. There had already been several confiscated by him in previous classes and David didn't want his to be next.

When the class was over, David was standing in the hallway about to pick up his messages when he noticed someone watching him. It was Bronx.

"I think it's about time you apologized to me," she said.

David had been avoiding her ever since their incident in the café. "I wasn't sure you'd ever talk to me again."

"Still waiting."

"You're right – I'm sorry. I was just trying to get to know more about you."

"No you weren't. You were gradin' me like I was just a profile on one of your stupid questionnaires."

David knew she was right. "I'm sorry."

"If you want to get to know me, you just have to spend more time with me."

"Is that still a possibility?"

"Maybe. Call me later and I'll let you know."

He watched as Bronx headed off to her next class. He would definitely be calling her later.

When he looked at his phone, he was surprised to see he had five missed calls from Professor Livingston, plus three voice-mails. The first voice-mail was the one where he said he knew who the second shooter was. The second voice-mail was a frantic message asking him to call him back. David listened to the third message.

"I've got the CD's, but I don't want to meet at the university. Someone might be watching. I'm going to sneak out a back door and I'll meet you at the bus stop at Sunview and University at eight tonight. Don't be late."

* * *

With each passing day of fall, the days were getting shorter and shorter. Even though it was only about five in the afternoon, it was already starting to get dark as Todd pulled into the almost deserted parking lot of a building alongside the University of Waterloo. He pulled out his Blackberry and noted that the logo on his phone matched the logo on the building he was parked beside.

He texted the following message: "*In position. Waiting for instructions.*"

It was only a few minutes later when his cellphone chirped. "*Sunview & University. 8:00 pm.*"

Todd started his car and drove to the intersection, scanning to look for the best place for him to set up. He circled the block a few times before making his decision.

The area around the two universities was experiencing a bit of a construction boom. Many of the small houses had been bought up by developers who were now in the process of putting up high-rise condos and apartment buildings in their place. Todd decided the best vantage point would be a relatively small building of about eight stories.

He pulled into the muddy construction site and parked beside a half-ton truck. Most of the construction workers were packing up for the day, although there were still a few around finishing up whatever they were working on.

When Todd got out of his car, he put on the coat he had brought with him to go hunting. It didn't look much different than the clothes the construction workers were wearing.

"Time to call it a day," one of the workers said as he threw his gear into the back of the half-ton. His buddy did the same and then climbed into the passenger side. When they backed up, they didn't notice Todd grab the hard-hat from the back of their truck and put it on.

There were a bunch of discarded steel studs piled a few feet away. Todd went over and grabbed a few of them. He did a quick look around to make sure no one was watching and then opened his trunk. He pulled the steel gun case out and placed it with the steel studs. Then he picked them all up, threw them over his shoulder and walked into the building. He looked just like any of the other workers carting material around.

There were a few workers in the steel hoist coming down from the upper floors of the building as Todd approached. They opened the cage door and filed out with their gear. One of them held the door open for Todd to get in.

"Hold up," a man yelled as he approached the hoist. He climbed in and hit the button for the sixth floor. "What level?"

"Four," Todd said.

The hoist lurched and then squealed as it started the ascent. When they got to the fourth level, the man opened the gate for Todd. "Don't be too long. The supervisor will be around to shut everything down in about twenty minutes."

"I've just got a few things to finish up," Todd said.

As he walked around, he was pleased to see that the fourth floor was abandoned, although he could still hear work going being done on the floors above him. He headed over to the side of the building that faced the University-Sunview intersection and determined that his sight lines were pretty much perfect. However, lighting was going to be a problem. The building was lit up like a Christmas tree with construction lights and Todd didn't want anyone to see him.

He found a place he could hide until the rest of the

construction workers left. Gradually there was less and less noise on the floors above him as the workers headed home for the day. He heard the hoist coming down and was alarmed when it stopped on his level. "Anybody still here?" he heard someone yell. As he peeked over the pile of construction materials he had hidden behind, Todd could see it was the supervisor making his last round. Todd didn't make a sound.

He watched as the supervisor flipped the breaker to turn off the construction lights. Suddenly the floor went dark, except for a few lights near the elevator. He watched the supervisor get into the hoist and head down to the third floor, where he repeated the procedure. Over the next twenty minutes, the construction site got darker and quieter until there wasn't any sound at all.

Perfect. Now Todd could prepare for his assignment. He carried his gun case over to the side of the building facing the intersection, opened the case and pulled the rifle out. Then he attached the site to the rifle and verified that he had a good view of the location.

Now all he had to do was wait.

* * *

David threw his soccer bag over his shoulder and walked the few blocks from his residence to the intersection where the professor said he wanted to meet. There weren't a lot of people out on the street at this time. Students who had evening classes were already there as they typically went from seven to ten. Since it was a cool night, there weren't many people heading out just for a walk. Everyone who was out this night had a purpose.

David saw a bus pull away as he approached the stop, so there wasn't anyone else waiting. He sat on the bench that had a huge picture of a local real estate agent on it. He saw a blond woman across the street walking her dog, growing more and more impatient as she waited for the dog to do his business. There was no sign of the professor.

When he looked down the street, he could see someone approaching. At first, he thought it was the professor, but as he got closer he realized it was just a student. The hoodie and the backpack were a dead giveaway.

The professor was late.

* * *

Bronx was on her way back from doing some shopping. She normally walked everywhere, but had decided to take the bus back to the residence because it was a cool night and she didn't want to have to lug the bags all that way. She was getting close to her stop so she was starting to gather up her things.

The bus started to slow down and stopped to pick up a student who was waiting on the bench, but he waved the driver on.

"Are you sure?" the bus driver yelled as he opened the door. "This is the only bus running this time of night. The express buses quit at six."

"Yeah, sorry. I'm not waiting for a bus – I'm just meeting someone here."

Bronx looked out of the bus window and was surprised to see that it was David. "Wait!" she yelled to the driver. "I'd like to get off."

The bus driver opened the rear doors of the bus and Bronx scrambled to get off.

"David – where you headin' off to?"

He was surprised to see her. "Nowhere. I'm just meeting someone here."

She plopped down on the bench beside him. "Mind if I wait with you?"

"Ahh – it's probably not a good idea."

She studied his face. "If you're meetin' some girl, you can just tell me, yunno."

"I'm not meeting a girl."

"Good, then you won't mind me waitin' with you."

"It's probably best if you go," David persisted. "He's already late. Maybe he won't show at all."

Bronx looked worried. "Are you getting' yourself into trouble again?"

"No. It's nothing." David could see someone approaching. "That's probably him now. You should go."

Bronx saw the man approaching as well. "Okay, if you say so."

Bronx started to walk away, but she kept looking back over her shoulder. She watched David talk to the man and she saw him give something to David, but she couldn't see what it was. She looked ahead and saw someone wearing a hoodie coming toward her. Something wasn't right – she could feel it. She turned and started to run back toward David.

As he was opening his soccer bag, David looked up to see Bronx racing back toward him. He could also see the person who had walked by him earlier – the student in the hoodie with the backpack – coming up behind Bronx. He was pulling something out of his backpack.

David turned to the professor. "We've got to get out of here." He noticed a red dot dancing across the professor's chest. He had no idea what it was.

But being the daughter of a New York cop, Bronx knew exactly what it was. "Gun!!!" she screamed.

A gunshot pierced the air and David watched the professor fall to the ground. He froze in disbelief.

A second gunshot rang out as Bronx tackled him to the ground. As he lay there with Bronx on top of him, David knew he had been shot, yet he couldn't feel anything. He felt numb.

He heard someone shuffling around him, picking up the CDs the professor had given him that were now scattered all over the ground. Then the man in the hoodie stood over him, aiming the automatic pistol directly at his head. Their eyes locked and David was sure he was about to be executed. He closed his eyes.

He heard a third gunshot and then everything went silent. That's the last thing he remembered.

* * *

"Dammit – dammit – dammit," Todd said as he pulled out his cellphone and dialed 9-1-1.

"9-1-1. What is your emergency? Police, fire or ambulance?"

"I need an ambulance at the corner of University and Sunview immediately."

"Is this a car accident?"

"No. There's been a shooting."

"What is your name and location, sir?"

Todd ended the call without answering and then quickly packed his rifle into the gun case. As he surveyed the scene, he saw the lady with the dog cross the street to check on the victims. A bus heading in the other direction slammed on the brakes and the driver ran off the bus carrying his emergency kit.

Todd heard the sound of sirens approaching. There was nothing more he could do. It was time for him to get out of there.

*** CHAPTER 23 ***

Laura was reading the newspaper while she sat in the waiting room at the hospital. *"Two Dead, Two Injured in Waterloo Shooting"* the headlines read. Henry was pacing back and forth, looking at the doors into the Intensive Care Unit every few seconds. They had flown back from Chicago as soon as they'd received the call – the call that no parent ever wants to receive.

The newspaper didn't have many details at this point, but the few they had were shocking. *"Professor Nigel Livingston, of the University of Waterloo, was shot and killed while he waited for a bus at the intersection of University Avenue and Sunview Street in Waterloo at approximately 8:30 p.m. last night. A second unidentified man was also shot and killed. Heather Low and David Shaw, both first year students at Wilfrid Laurier University, were also shot in the incident and are in critical condition in hospital. Police do not have a motive for the shooting at this stage, but indicated they are still in the preliminary stages of their investigation."* The article continued, but it mostly consisted of background information and speculation as to whether the shooting was a possible terrorist attack.

"Dad, you should come and sit down," Robert said. "They said we wouldn't hear anything more about David's surgery for at least two more hours." Robert had been at the hospital all night. He went over to give his father a hug. "I'm sure he'll be okay."

"Why is it taking so long?" Henry asked.

Robert escorted his father back to the seat beside him. "They said he's stable, but they don't want to operate to remove the bullet until they can reduce the swelling. They may not have even started his surgery yet." Robert had delivered the same message to his father several times already.

When the doors to the ICU opened and a nurse came out pushing a stretcher, everyone in the waiting room sprang from their chairs.

"Heather," a man said when he recognized the person on the stretcher. He was a big man with broad shoulders and a square jaw, wearing the uniform of a New York City cop.

"Are you her father?" the nurse asked.

"Yes. Is she going to be okay?"

Heather's mother tiptoed toward the stretcher as if she was almost afraid to look.

"She's going to be fine," the nurse said to both of them. "The bullet went right through her and didn't strike any vital organs. She's a lucky girl."

Another man elbowed his way up close to the stretcher. He was middle-aged, but the lines on his face made him appear much older. The faded brown sports-jacket he was wearing looked like it hadn't been dry-cleaned in over a year. "I'm Detective Tremblay," he said to the nurse. "When will she be ready to answer questions?"

"She should be fully conscious again within the next hour or so, but you'll have to keep it short. She needs her rest."

They all watched as the nurse pushed her stretcher down the hall to the recovery room. Heather's father walked alongside the stretcher, holding his daughter's hand the entire way. Her mother, a petite woman, held onto the other side of the stretcher, looking as if she would fall down if she let go.

Henry approached the nurse when she was on her way back to the ICU. "Any update on my son?"

"The swelling has gone down. They're just prepping him for surgery now. We should know within the next few hours." She reached out and touched Henry's arm. "I'm sure he'll be fine."

Henry resumed his pacing.

* * *

It was almost two hours later when the detective made his way into Bronx's room. He introduced himself to her parents and obtained permission to talk to their daughter.

"Miss Low, I'm Detective Tremblay. I was wondering if I could ask you a few questions."

She looked surprisingly good for someone who had just come out of surgery. "Sure. Do-ya know if David is okay?"

The detective pulled out a notepad and a pen from his pocket. "I believe he's still in surgery. Did you see who did the shooting?"

"I think so. He was wearin' a hoodie and had a backpack, but I didn't get a good look at his face."

The detective was confused. The guy in the hoodie was dead. They thought he was one of the victims. He pulled a picture out of his pocket and showed it to her. "Is this the man you think did the shooting?"

"Yeah, that's him. Did-ya catch him?"

The detective didn't answer. "Let's start over. Why don't you tell us what happened from the beginning?"

Bronx could tell the detective had doubts about what she had said. She looked over to her father for help. He took her hand to comfort her. "It's okay. Just tell the detective what you saw."

"Well, I was on the bus comin' back from shoppin' when I saw David at the bus stop, so I got off. He said he was waitin' to meet someone and I offered to wait with him, but he kept tryin' to get rid of me."

She looked at her father, who encouraged her to continue.

"I figured he was waitin' for a girl, so I started to leave. When I looked back, I saw a man givin' somethin' to David."

The detective pulled a picture of the professor from his pocket. "Is this the man that you saw give something to David?"

"Yes, that's him. Who is he?"

"His name is Nigel Livingston. He's a professor at Waterloo. Did you see what the professor gave David?"

"Not really. It mighta been some CDs, but I can't say for sure."

The detective continued to take notes. "Go on."

"Then I saw the man in the hoodie comin'. I just knew he was going to hurt David. I don't know how – I just knew it – so I started to run back toward David. That's when I saw it."

"Saw what?" the detective asked.

"The red laser-thingy of a gun. Ya-know, like the ones on TV." She looked at her father. "Like the ones your SWAT guys use."

The detective continued to take notes, but it wasn't making sense. They hadn't found a gun at the scene or any

CDs. "And then what happened?"

"I yelled *gun* when I saw the laser-thingy on the professor's chest. Then he got shot. I tried to knock David out of the way. That's the last thing I remember. I guess that's when I got shot."

Bronx started to cry. Her father leaned in to hug her.

"I think that's enough questions for now," the nurse said. "We should let her get some rest."

The detective picked up the pictures he had shown her and put them back into his pocket along with his notepad. "Thank you, Miss Low. You've been a big help." He turned to leave.

"Will you let me know if David is okay?"

The detective looked at the nurse. "I'll let you know when I know."

* * *

Detective Tremblay went to the end of the hallway and called his chief to report his findings. "The girl says the guy in the hoodie was the shooter, but that doesn't make any sense. Do we have an ID on him yet?"

"No," the chief said. "It's really strange. He had no identification on him whatsoever. We've run his fingerprints through the system and got nothing. If he really was the shooter, you'd think he'd be in the system somewhere."

"The girl said she saw him pull a handgun from his backpack and saw a laser sight on the professor's chest before he was shot."

"That sounds like a Crimson Trace laser sight," the chief said, "and that's only used by pros. Do you think there's any way this was a professional hit?"

"I find that hard to believe, but this whole case doesn't add up. If he really was the shooter, then where's his gun?

We didn't find any weapons at the scene. And who the hell shot him?"

"Hold on," the chief said. There was a pause of a few seconds. "You're not going to believe this. The M.E. just handed me a report saying the bullet they pulled from the guy in the hoodie doesn't match the bullet that killed the professor. It was a 5.56mm bullet – the kind used in military rifles. You know what that means."

They were both thinking the same thing.

There was a second shooter.

*** CHAPTER 24 ***

It was almost four hours later when the nurse wheeled David out of the Intensive Care Unit. David's grandmother and his Aunt Jenny had now joined the rest of his family waiting to hear how he was doing.

Henry was still pacing back and forth when the doors opened, but his knees buckled when he saw David's swollen face and the bandages around his head. Robert caught his father before he hit the floor.

"How is he?" Robert asked the nurse.

"He's a very lucky man," she said. "It was touch and go there for a while, but the surgeon managed to successfully remove the bullet from the base of his skull."

Henry almost threw up. "He got shot in the head?"

"The bullet actually entered his chest just below the collarbone, exited out of the top of his shoulder and then re-entered along the side of his neck. We believe this was the same bullet that went through Miss Low. She was found lying on top of your son at the scene."

"My daughter said she was trying to push him out of the way," said Bronx's father.

The nurse turned to him. "She probably saved his life."

"When will he be awake?" Henry asked.

"We put him into a medically induced coma for the surgery," the nurse said. "It will probably be a few more hours."

Henry couldn't believe what he was hearing. "He's in a coma?"

The nurse reached out to comfort Henry. "Yes. We gave him some drugs to put him into a coma, but just for the surgery. It's a lot safer that way. Once the swelling goes down, we'll be bringing him out of it."

The nurse wheeled the stretcher to a special recovery room and began hooking David up to a myriad of monitors that tracked every vital sign, including an EEG to track his brain activity. There was hardly any activity, with only periodic pulses. The entire family hovered outside the door, watching and waiting.

"I'm sorry," the nurse said, "but you'll have to go back to the waiting room. There's not enough room in here for you. There's nothing you can do and it will be several hours until we decide to wake him up."

Henry noticed there was one chair in the room. "Are you sure I can't stay with my son?"

The nurse could see the concern on his face. "Okay, but just you. The rest of you will have to go back to the waiting room."

Henry sat in the chair and looked at all of the monitors that hummed and beeped. He had no idea what any of them did.

"He's going to be okay," the nurse reassured him as she left the room.

As Henry sat there, he found himself rocking back and forth to the sound of the machines. It felt as if his own heartbeat fell into the same rhythm as his son's.

* * *

"Mr. Shaw," the nurse said as she gently touched Henry's arm.

Henry awoke with a start to see the room now had several doctors and nurses in attendance. "What's wrong? Is David okay?"

"Yes, he's fine," the nurse reassured him. "The swelling has gone down and we're going to bring him out of the coma now. We thought it would be best if you were the first person he saw when he opened his eyes."

The nurse helped Henry from his chair and held him as they stood alongside the bed. He watched as one of the doctors injected something into David's IV. Within a few seconds, the EEG was showing more and more activity. The other monitors also increased their beeping.

It was only a few seconds later when David opened his eyes. "Hey, Dad."

Tears began to stream down Henry's face. "Hi, son. It's good to have you back."

David's eyes scanned the faces of the strangers who were all watching him. "Where am I?"

"You're in the hospital," Henry said.

"David," one of the doctors said. "Could you tell us when your birthday is?"

David paused. "May 13th."

"And what school do you go to?"

"Wilfrid Laurier." David was confused as to why they were asking him these questions.

"What was the name of your first pet?"

David had to think for a second. "Duddly."

The doctor looked at Henry for confirmation. "Yes, Duddly was the name of our dog."

The doctor smiled at David. "I'm just asking you these

questions to check your memory." He patted David on the shoulder. "And it appears that you're doing just fine. Congratulations."

"I was just having the strangest dream," David said. "Duddly was licking my face. I kept trying to get him to stop, but he wouldn't. He just kept licking and licking."

Henry looked concerned. "Duddly died a few years ago. You remember that, right?"

"Of course I do," David said.

"That's nothing to worry about," the doctor said. "People have been known to have some strange dreams when they're coming out of anesthetic. David, we're going to unhook you from all of these machines now and move you to another room. But you're going to be in the hospital for a while yet. You've been through quite a bit and you're going to have to take it slow for a while."

"Okay," David said.

"Do you have any questions before I go?"

As David thought, he suddenly started to remember the shooting and the panic spread across his face. "Is Bronx okay?"

The doctor looked confused.

The nurse leaned in to whisper to the doctor. "Bronx is the nickname of the girl who was shot."

"I'm not at liberty to say," the doctor said.

The nurse could see the concern on David's face. "She's fine," the nurse whispered to David when the doctor turned away. "She's probably going to be released within the next few days."

David sighed in relief.

As the doctor exited the room, he was approached by Detective Tremblay. "Is it okay if I ask him some questions?"

The doctor looked back at David. "The anesthetic

might affect some of his memories for a while yet. I'd give him another day if I were you."

* * *

The detective called his chief. "The Shaw kid is awake and it looks like he's going to make it, but the doctor doesn't want me to talk to him until tomorrow."

"Does he know we've got another potential murderer out there on the street?"

"No, I haven't shared any of our findings yet. The doc said the anesthetic they gave him might mess up his memory for a while. I'll try to talk to him again first thing in the morning."

The chief sighed in frustration. "We just got word that the professor's office was broken into. They did a real number on it – trashed all of the computers and took a bunch of stuff."

"Do you think it was the guy in the hoodie?"

"Not possible. The prof's assistant said everything was fine when he left the office at ten, and the guy in the hoodie was already dead by then."

"Have we got an ID on him yet?"

"No," the chief said. "And we might never get one."

"Why not?"

"The body's gone. Someone stole it right out of the morgue. We're checking the security tapes as we speak to try to figure out who took it."

"This case just keeps getting stranger and stranger," the detective said.

"We better get someone to watch the Shaw kid. If someone wanted him dead, they might make another attempt. I'll send over a uniform to camp outside his room."

"I'll watch him until he gets here. No one will get to the

kid on my watch."

* * *

Robert was totally exhausted when he climbed out of the taxi in front of the residence. It was only about seven in the evening but he'd been up for over twenty-four hours straight. Now that he knew David was going to be okay, he was hoping to get some sleep. As he approached the elevators, he was surprised to see Vanessa sitting in the cafeteria. She came out when she saw him.

"How's your brother?"

"He's going to be okay. They got the bullet out, but it was really scary there for a while."

Vanessa gave him a hug. "I'm so glad. You look exhausted."

"I am. I'm going to go crash, but I want to go back to the hospital again first thing in the morning."

Vanessa grabbed his arm. "Let me help. You look like you could fall down any minute." She continued to hold his arm as they rode up in the elevator. "You're a good guy, you know. You and your brother don't deserve any of this."

When they got to W308, Robert was alarmed to see that the door wasn't locked. He was even more alarmed when he pushed the door open and saw the chaos inside.

"Oh my God," Vanessa said. She started to walk inside, but Robert pulled her back and quickly dialed 9-1-1 on his cellphone. The police were there in a matter of minutes.

* * *

"The only things they took were our computers," Robert said to Detective Tremblay a few hours later.

The detective could tell this was not a typical robbery. It was obvious that the room had been completely searched, yet no one in the residence had seen or heard anything.

"We're going to dust for fingerprints," the detective said, "but I don't think we're going to find anything." They hadn't found any clues at the professor's office and he was sure he'd come up with the same result here. These guys were pros. Evidence was disappearing at an alarming rate – the weapons from the shooting – the CDs or whatever the professor had given David – even a body from the morgue.

"Do you have a place you can stay for the night?" the detective asked Robert.

Vanessa grabbed Robert's arm. "You can stay at my place if you want," she whispered to him.

"Thanks, but I'll probably just get a room at the hotel. That's where my Dad and the rest of my family are staying. I sort of want to be around family right now."

"I understand," Vanessa said.

"I'll have one of the officers drive you," Detective Tremblay said as he waved one of them over. "I'll see you at the hospital in the morning. I plan to interview your brother first thing."

* * *

David was starting to look more like himself again. His face had regained a healthy pinkish tone and the swelling on the side of his neck and head had gone down substantially. In fact, he had asked for something to eat, but the nurse had refused. "Not yet," she said. "You're getting everything you need right now through the IV."

The whole family had come to the hospital that morning to see David, but the nurse had only let Henry in so far. "He still needs a lot of rest, so we've got to take things slow," she said. She also knew that Detective Tremblay would be arriving soon to question him.

"How are you doing this morning?" the detective said

when he arrived a few minutes later.

"Pretty good, except that I'm starving."

"That's a good sign. That means you're getting better. Do you feel up to answering a few questions?"

"Sure," David said.

The detective pulled a notepad and pen from his pocket. "We understand that you were meeting the professor at the bus stop to get something from him. Can you tell me what that was?"

"Some CDs."

"What was on the CDs?"

David looked at his father. He knew that his father had told him not to have anything more to do with the secret society because it was too dangerous. "Sorry, Dad."

"It was some files that I had given to the professor to hang onto," David said to the detective. David proceeded to tell him about the secret society and how he had been arrested by the FBI in Chicago. "The files were encrypted, but the professor had cracked it. He was bringing me a copy of the unencrypted files."

"What was in the files?"

"I don't know. I never did see them, but they apparently have something to do with the Kennedy assassination. The professor told me the files showed who really killed the President."

The detective stopped writing. If that was true, he knew they were in way over their heads. Was this kid telling the truth or just suffering from a severe blow to the head? It would explain a lot of things – whoever had shot them and then made the evidence disappear were professionals.

"Before we go down that path, let's focus on who shot you and the professor. Did you see who that was?"

"I think it was the guy in the hoodie. The professor had just handed me the CDs when he got shot. Is he okay?"

No one had told David what had happened to the professor. "I'm sorry," the detective said. "He didn't make it."

The colour drained from David's face.

"Is the guy in the hoodie the one that shot you?" the detective continued.

"I think so," David said. "Bronx had yelled that he had a gun and she was trying to push me out of the way. She's okay, right?"

"Yes, she's fine. We think the same bullet went through her before it hit you. Do you remember anything else?"

"I remember lying on the ground. I knew I'd been shot, but I couldn't move or feel anything. I heard someone gathering up the CDs and then the guy in the hoodie was standing over me. He pointed his gun right at my head. I closed my eyes and then I heard the gunshot."

David turned to his father. "How am I not dead?"

Henry looked as pale as his son. "Someone shot the guy in the hoodie."

"Who?" David asked, looking back at the detective.

"We don't know. But we know he was killed with a different gun than the one that was used to shoot you and the professor. Do you remember anyone else being there?"

David thought as he relived the incident again. "There was a lady across the street walking her dog." David turned to his father. "That's who was licking my face. That wasn't a dream – it wasn't Duddly – it was *her* dog that was licking my face. I couldn't move, so I couldn't get him to stop."

The detective had no record of the lady. According to their investigation, the first person on the scene after the shooting was the bus driver – the one who had rushed over with the emergency kit.

"Do you remember anything about this lady?" the detective asked.

"She was blond – I remember that – but she was across the street so I didn't get a good look at her face. But she was there after the shooting because I remember the dog licking my face."

"Do you remember anything else?"

David thought again. "She said something."

"She spoke to you?"

"I don't know if she was talking to me or not – maybe to the guy in the hoodie – she said *I'm sorry – you didn't deserve this*. That's the last thing I remember."

"You've been a great help," the detective said. "I'll let you get some rest now, but just let the nurse know if you remember anything else. I won't be far away."

Finally, he had a lead. The lady with the dog was probably the person who had removed the gun and the CDs from the scene. But if she was involved, why would she have shot her partner? Something still didn't add up.

Detective Tremblay walked down the hall to call in the results of his interview to the chief. "I just interviewed the Shaw kid. It appears that whoever wanted the CDs sent an entire team for the job. He said there was a blond lady with a dog that gathered up the CDs and the gun after the shooting."

"Is she the one who shot the guy in the hoodie?"

"I don't think so," the detective said. "The M.E. said he was shot with a rifle. There's no way she'd be out walking her dog with a rifle on her hip – it would be too conspicuous. This was a professional hit. I think she was there just to clean things up."

"Do you think the kid is still in danger?"

"I don't know," the detective said. "If they wanted him dead, the lady with the dog could have easily killed him. Maybe all they wanted was the files back."

"So, if she didn't shoot the guy in the hoodie, who did?"

"We don't know – probably a professional sniper. The bullet they pulled from him wasn't a normal bullet. It was the kind used only by a military or police marksman."

*** CHAPTER 25 ***

It was around noon a few days later when Bronx was released from hospital. Her father was pushing her out in a wheelchair.

"Can we make a stop before we leave?" Bronx asked her father.

"Sure. What do you need?"

"I'd like to stop and say goodbye to David before we go."

Her father stopped at the desk and asked one of the nurses for David's room number. David sat up in bed when he saw them at his door.

"What are you doing in a wheelchair? Are you okay?"

"I'm fine. They just have some silly rule that patients must leave in a wheelchair. I think it's just so they don't get sued if you fall down on the way out." She turned to her father as she got out of the wheelchair. "Dad, can you give us a minute?"

"I'll be just down the hall, but don't be long. We've got a long trip ahead of us."

Bronx went over to the side of the bed and gently

touched the bandages on David's neck and head. David reached out and held her arm.

"A long trip? Where you going?"

"My dad's takin' me back to New Yawk. Says I'd actually be safer back in the Bronx. It was hard to argue with him sportin' a bullet hole in my chest."

"What about school?"

"I was probably gonna flunk out anyway. This just gives me a good excuse to start over. My dad wants me to enroll in Brooklyn College next year – says it's *the poor man's Harvard*."

David could not hide his disappointment. "I was hoping that maybe we could…"

Bronx didn't let him finish. "When you're up and about again, you should come see me in New Yawk. I could show you around. I think you'd love it."

"I might just do that." David smiled at her. "But I hear it can be a pretty dangerous city. Who's going to watch my back when I'm there?"

"Me, stupid. I already told ya – in the Bronx, we watch each other's backs."

David held her hand. "Yeah, I know. The doc said you probably saved my life when you pushed me to the ground. Thanks."

"It was nuthin. But you're gonna have to stay out of trouble once I'm gone. I wouldn't want anythin' to happen to ya."

Bronx's father appeared in the doorway. "We should get going."

"Okay. I'm coming."

She gave David's face one last caress and started heading toward the door. Suddenly, she turned and raced back toward him and gave him a kiss. This wasn't a little peck on the cheek. It was a full open-mouth kiss that almost sucked

David's tonsils right out of his throat.

"Sorry," she said. "But I've been dyin' to do that for a long time."

Then she was gone.

* * *

It was a few hours later when Robert showed up at the hospital to visit his brother.

"She's gone," David said.

"Who's gone?"

"Bronx. She was released this morning. Her father took her back to New York – said she'd be safer there."

Robert could tell that his brother was upset. "I'm sorry to hear that. I could tell that you had a – a connection with her."

Robert wanted to change the topic to something more positive, but he had nothing. "I'm afraid I've got more bad news. Somebody broke into our room and stole our computers."

He didn't get a reaction from David. He could tell he was still thinking about Bronx. The silence was making Robert uncomfortable, so he just kept talking. "I've already gone down to the tech shop in the university bookstore. They sold me a brand new laptop – said I didn't have to pay for it until I get the money from the insurance company for the one that got stolen."

Again, nothing but silence.

"I need it for my classes," Robert continued. "Do you want me to get one for you?"

David seemed to suddenly realize he'd been asked a question. "Sorry, what?"

"Do you want me to get you a new laptop to replace your computer that got stolen?"

"I'm not sure," David said. "They say I might be in here

for a few more days. I've already missed a week of classes. I don't know how I'll ever catch up."

"I'm sure your profs will cut you some slack. Getting shot is a pretty good excuse for not handing in a few assignments on time."

The conversation about computers made David think about the one hidden in his soccer bag. "Do you know where my soccer bag is?"

"I have no idea. I don't remember seeing it at the residence."

"No. I had it with me at the bus stop when I got shot. Do you know what happened to it?"

"Well, if it was at the bus stop, the police probably have it."

"Either that, or the lady with the dog took it."

"Lady with a dog? What are you talking about?"

Robert hadn't been there when Detective Tremblay had questioned David about the shooting and nothing about her had been reported in the newspaper, so he was completely confused.

"Can you tell the detective I need to see him again? Go ask the nurse. She's got the number to call him."

Robert had no idea what was going on, but headed out to find the nurse.

"And ask him if he's got my soccer bag?" David yelled.

* * *

"I hear you may have remembered something else," Detective Tremblay said when he showed up at the hospital a few hours later.

David sat up in bed. "Good, you've got my soccer bag."

The detective put it on the corner of the bed. "Yes, we found the laptop hidden in the bottom of the bag, but the only fingerprints we found on it were yours." He handed

David the laptop. "What's on the computer?"

"Nothing. I just wondered if the lady with the dog took it."

"Apparently not. I have something I want you to look at." Detective Tremblay pulled some pictures out of his pocket. "These were taken by a security cam outside of a pub a few blocks away." He showed David the first one, which had a time-stamp of 7:46 p.m. and showed a blond lady with a dog. "Is this the lady you saw?"

The picture mostly showed the parking lot outside of the pub, so the picture of the lady walking on the sidewalk was pretty small.

"Yeah, I think so," David said.

The detective showed David another picture, this one a blown up image of just the lady. "Do you recognize her?"

Although the picture was a close-up, the pixilation of the photograph seemed to distort it. "She looks familiar, but I can't really say who she is."

"Take your time," the detective said.

David studied the photograph. "No, I don't know who it is."

"Well, she was definitely there at the time of the shooting. We have another picture of her walking back in the other direction at 8:41. That's a long walk for such a small dog. And she's carrying a pretty big bag – big enough to hold a gun and some CDs. No one would carry a bag like that just to walk their dog."

"I think that's her," David said. "And I think that was the dog that was licking my face."

The detective gathered up the pictures and put them back inside his pocket. "Why don't you show me what's on the computer?"

David wasn't sure he should. "I don't think it will work without an Internet connection."

"I'm sure we can find one," the detective said. He went to the door and waved to the nurse. "Where's the nearest Internet connection?"

"None of these workstations have it," the nurse said, pointing at the computers at the nurse's station, "but there's one just down the hall. We use it all the time."

"Feel like a little walk?" the detective asked David.

David sensed that *no* wasn't the answer the detective was looking for. He started to get out of bed. Since the shooting, he'd only walked the few steps to get up to go to the bathroom and that was with a nurse holding on to him.

When the nurse saw him getting up, she came racing over. "I'm not sure this is a good idea."

"I'm sure he'll be fine," the detective said. "David here was just saying how he felt like stretching his legs."

The detective grabbed the laptop in one hand and held onto David with the other. The nurse grabbed David's other arm as they helped him walk down the hallway to the little alcove where there was a computer with an Internet connection.

"I think we'll be okay from here," the detective said to the nurse after they helped David sit down.

The nurse wasn't sure if she should leave or not.

"I'm fine," David reassured her.

After she left, David asked the detective to pull the Internet cable from the back of the computer that was there. Then he plugged the cable into his laptop.

As soon as he turned on the computer, it prompted for a password. David stopped to think, and then hummed the limerick to himself that he had created to help him remember it. When he hit the enter key, the computer continued its startup sequence.

"*Negotiating protocol…*"

"*Securing communications channel…*"

After a few more seconds, "*Welcome, Goliath*" appeared on the screen.

"Who's Goliath?" the detective asked.

"I am," David said. "That's my code name."

"*Retrieve instructions*," David typed.

After a few seconds, a message appeared on the screen.

"*Watch out for the second shooter.*"

"What does that mean?" the detective asked.

"Not really sure, but I think it was telling us to look for the second shooter in the files that the U.S. government released about the Kennedy assassination. The professor said he'd looked at the files – said he knew who the second shooter was."

"That's probably why they killed him – and tried to kill you."

David looked at the detective. "Now, that they've got the CDs back, do you think they're still going to try to kill me?"

"I don't know. If they really wanted you dead, the lady with the dog could have finished the job. But I'm going to leave an officer outside of your room here until we know for sure. You never actually looked at those files, did you?"

"No, but maybe they think I did."

"I'll try to figure out a way to get the word out that you don't know what was in the files. Maybe that will take the heat off you. I'll try to leak something to the press."

"I know," David said. "My dad's girlfriend is a reporter – with the Chicago Tribune. I'm sure she'd help – she already helped me when I was in Chicago."

* * *

"I was wondering if you and your girlfriend would mind coming over to the hospital," Detective Tremblay said when he called Henry. "We need your help with something."

"Is David okay?"

"Yes, he's recovering just fine."

Henry was confused. "Laura was just about to head to the airport to fly back to Chicago. Why do you need her there?"

"I'll explain everything when you get here. It's important."

Henry and Laura showed up about half an hour later. "What's going on?" Henry asked from the doorway.

Detective Tremblay waved for them to move into David's room and closed the door behind them. "We're not sure, but we think there's a chance there may be another attempt on David's life."

Henry looked shocked. "Why?"

"We think this whole thing was a professional hit related to some files pertaining to the Kennedy assassination. The professor told David that he had decrypted the files and that's why they were meeting – so the professor could give David the CDs. Whoever shot them, took the CDs."

"So if they got what they were after, why would David still be in danger?"

"Because they may think David saw what was in the files. The professor told David he had looked at the files and knew who the second shooter was. We think that's why the professor was killed."

Henry looked at David. "Do you know what was in the files?"

"No. But they don't know that."

"That's why we think David may still be in danger," the detective said.

Henry looked like he was going to faint. "So what are we going to do?"

The detective looked at Laura. "We need someone to

leak the fact that David never saw what was in those files."

Laura suddenly realized why she had been invited to this meeting. "And you want that person to be me."

"Precisely," the detective said. "But it has to look like you found out this information all on your own. If they know I fed it to you, they'll never believe it and they may still come after David."

"I don't like it," Henry said. "You have to protect David."

"We will," the detective said. "But we can't protect him for the rest of his life. They'll keep coming for him as long as they think he knows what's in those files."

Laura reached over to comfort Henry. "He's right. In my research for this story, there's been a lot of potential witnesses who have died mysterious deaths – hit and runs – weird explosions."

"Do you think you can write the story without making it look like a plant?" the detective asked.

"I'm sure of it," Laura said, "but I'll have to name David as my source to give the story any kind of credibility. You'll also have to give me something that no one else knows – something not already given to the local press."

David looked at the detective. "The lady with the dog."

* * *

Laura camped out in David's room for the next few hours while she wrote the story. She showed it to the detective when she was done.

"I think this will work," Detective Tremblay said. "How quickly can we get this in the papers?"

"I'm going to call my editor now, but I'm pretty sure this will be front page material. He's pissed at me right now because he thinks I've let the stories we've been running on the JFK conspiracy die when I came up here. He'll wet himself when he sees this. Is there a place around here where I can send this to him?"

"There sure is," the detective said.

He led Laura down the hall to the little alcove with the computer and the Internet connection. Laura unplugged the cable from the computer and plugged it into her laptop. She sent the story to the Tribune and then called her editor to let him know it was there.

"He says it'll run front page tomorrow," Laura said to the detective when she ended the call with her editor.

"Great," Detective Tremblay said. "I hope this works."

As Laura bent down to put the Internet cable back into the computer, she glanced down the hallway and was caught by surprise by what she saw. She was sure that it was Todd talking to one of the nurses. She bumped her head on the side of the computer stand as she quickly tried to stand up. When she looked down the hallway again, he was gone.

*** CHAPTER 26 ***

"Professional Hit Tied to JFK Assassination" the headline read in the Tribune the next day. The story had been picked up by several newsfeeds so it also appeared in multiple newspapers across the U.S. and Canada.

It was a brilliant piece of journalism. It described how four people had been gunned down by professional assassins, how the mysterious *"lady with a dog"* had scooped up the murder weapon and the CDs containing information about who actually killed JFK and vanished into the night. It also told how the body of one of the assassins had been stolen from the morgue.

The main source for the story was identified as David Shaw, one of the victims of the shooting, who the reporter had secretly interviewed while he recovered in hospital. It described how Professor Nigel Livingston had viewed the files that showed who actually killed JFK, but how the assassins had ended his life before he could show the files to David, and now David wondered, along with the rest of the world, what actually happened on that November day in Dallas, 1963. The story had quotes from Detective

Tremblay denying the validity of any of the facts reported in the story and simply stating that their investigation was ongoing.

In subsequent TV interviews, Detective Tremblay played his part perfectly by being "*visibly upset*" that anything had been leaked to the press. The detective hoped his performance would convince the assassins that David posed no further threat to them.

There was even a TV interview of a very embarrassed chief of police denying that a body had gone missing from the morgue. That part wasn't acting at all. Detective Tremblay hadn't informed the chief of the plan, something that he was sure would be discussed in detail at his next performance appraisal.

"Do you think it worked?" Henry asked the detective.

"I'm not sure. I'm going to leave an officer on duty here at the hospital to watch over David for the next few days. If David does know anything about the JFK assassination, they'll wonder why he didn't already tell the press. Hopefully, they'll conclude that he doesn't have anything to tell and they'll let him get on with his life."

The detective turned to Laura. "Thanks for your help. You may have saved David's life."

"I think you deserve most of the credit, for coming up with the plan in the first place. All I did was write the story."

As Laura was heading out of the hospital, she noticed one of the nurses filling in a patient's chart at the station. She was sure it was the same nurse she had seen the night before.

"Can I help you?" the nurse asked.

"I saw you talking to a man in the hallway here last night. Can I ask who that was?"

The nurse looked confused. "I'm not sure who you're

referring to. We get a lot of people through here."

"He was tall, just over six feet tall – dark hair."

The nurse still looked confused.

"*Very* good looking," Laura added.

"Oh, *him*," the nurse said, her face flushing a little bit. "Yes, I remember him. He didn't give a name. He was asking about David Shaw's condition – said he was a friend of the family. Is there a problem?"

Laura looked concerned. "I'm not sure."

* * *

"I'm sorry," Detective Tremblay said to the chief. The detective had been called in to explain how the information about the missing body from the morgue had been leaked to the press. "It would have come out eventually anyway. I thought it might help save the kid's life."

"You made our whole department look like the *Keystone Cops*," the chief said as he stomped around his office. "Now I've got to explain how a fucking dead guy got up and walked out of the morgue without anyone noticing."

"I'm sorry," Detective Tremblay said again. "Do we know how they actually pulled it off?"

"Some blond lady showed up and said they needed to do a second autopsy – said they might have missed something in the first one. She showed ID saying she was from the Coroner's office. She signed the body out – it all appeared legit." The chief sat down at his desk and put his head in his hands. "We've even got a security cam picture of her – except the Coroner says he's never seen her before in his life."

"Can I see the picture?"

The chief opened the file on his desk, pulled out the picture and threw it at the detective.

As soon as he saw it, the detective knew who it was.

"That's the lady from the crime scene – the lady who took the murder weapon and the CDs – the lady with the dog."

"Are you sure? This lady looks twenty years older than the one with the dog."

The detective pulled the picture of the lady with the dog from his coat pocket and placed the two pictures side-by-side. "She must be wearing makeup to make herself look older, but look – look at the hair – it's identical. It's obviously a wig."

The chief took a closer look at both pictures. "We *are* the fucking *Keystone Cops.*"

* * *

David was getting restless. He was feeling better and better with each passing day, but he was also bored to tears. "Are your sure you can't get me a TV or an Internet connection?" David asked the nurse.

"I've already told you – this is a recovery room. You can only get those things in regular rooms on the ward. You're lucky – most people that are in here are unconscious."

"Then can you move me to a regular room?"

"No, the police have said you're supposed to stay put until they say otherwise."

David threw himself back onto his bed. "Do you think I could take my laptop down to that alcove down the hall, so I could use the Internet connection there?"

The nurse was growing tired of David's whining. "Let me ask."

David watched as the nurse spoke to the officer stationed outside of David's room. He saw her point to the alcove that was only about twenty paces down the hall.

"He said you can – but he has to go with you," the nurse said to David when she came back into his room.

David sprang from the bed and grabbed his laptop.

"Take it slow," the nurse cautioned. "You might feel a bit dizzy when you get up."

David had already been out of bed several times and paced back and forth in his room just to relieve the boredom. "I'm fine."

The police officer escorted David the short distance down the hall. When he got there, he unplugged the Internet cable from the workstation and plugged it into his laptop.

"*Retrieve instructions*," David typed after he had entered his password.

"*Danger. Watch out for the second shooter*," appeared on the screen.

Why would he still be in danger? The newspaper reports had indicated he didn't know what was in the files. It didn't make any sense.

It had been a few days since he had read his messages. Maybe this was an old message that was sent before the newspaper article appeared. He checked the timestamp on the message.

It had been sent less than an hour ago.

*** CHAPTER 27 ***

Vanessa hurried into calculus class and sat down beside Robert. "New laptop?"

"Yeah, I got a new one to replace the one that got stolen – got it at the university tech shop. I've gotta get another one for my brother."

"How's he doing?"

"He's fine."

"Everyone around here is spooked since the shooting – thinking there's some nut job still out there."

Robert leaned in to whisper to Vanessa. "The cops don't think it was some whacko who did it. Think it was actually a professional hit."

"Yeah, I read that in the paper. Anyway, I'm glad to hear your brother is okay."

"He's actually getting bored just lying around in the hospital. He's hoping to get out in the next day or so, but the cops want to keep him there to protect him."

"Why would he need protection? I read in the paper that he doesn't know anything."

"He doesn't, but the cops don't want to take any

chances."

The chatter in the lecture hall dropped significantly when the calculus professor arrived and threw his briefcase onto the desk at the front of the room.

"Hold on to your hat," Vanessa said. "The hurricane is about to start."

Sure enough, for the next hour the professor spewed his knowledge at a frightening pace. He showed no pity on those who couldn't keep up.

"I'm thinking of dropping this class," Vanessa said after the lecture was over. "I just can't keep up."

"You can't," Robert said. "Calculus is a required course."

"I know. I'm thinking of dropping out altogether. I'm not sure math is the field I should be in."

Robert was stunned. He really looked forward to calculus class, and Vanessa was the main reason. "Don't give up. Maybe I can help you."

"Our study group already meets twice a week. I don't think we could ask them to meet more than that."

"I don't mean the study group. Just you and me. One-on-one."

"You'd do that for me?"

"Sure I would. How about we start tonight?"

* * *

Robert showed up at Vanessa's place just before seven that night. She lived in a very tiny house not far from the university. There were several other houses on the block just like it – old, rundown. This was an investment property so the owner just did the minimum amount required – and students were used to living with the bare minimum.

When Robert knocked on the door, he heard a dog bark

and come racing to the door. When Vanessa opened the door, she tried to block the dog from getting out with her leg.

"Don't worry about him – he's harmless," she said as she took Robert's coat. "But he might lick you to death."

Robert knelt down to pet the dog. "He reminds me of the dog David and I had when we were kids – a Bijon – his name was Duddly. What's this guy's name?"

"Wiley. You've got to watch him. He always seems to be up to something."

"Come on – this guy? He's too cute to be up to no good."

Wiley started sniffing around the huge bag that Robert had brought with him.

"See, I told you," Vanessa said. "If you've got any food in there, he'll steal it in a flash."

Robert picked up the bag and carried it over to the dining room table. It was obvious that it wasn't used very often for eating as Vanessa had her books spread out all over it. Some of the books looked like they'd never been opened.

Robert pulled a bottle of wine and some chocolates out of the bag. "I find studying calculus goes a lot better with some wine and something to nibble on."

"Something to nibble on? Are you sure you're talking about the chocolates?"

Robert looked a little embarrassed. "Maybe – maybe not."

"That's an awfully big bag. Any chance there's an actual calculus book in there?"

"Ta-da," Robert said when he pulled a calculus study guide from the bag. "But I also have something else I have to get done tonight."

He pulled a brand new laptop from the bag, along with a

bunch of other technical paraphernalia. "I picked up a new laptop for David today, but I have to set it up for him tonight. I promised I'd bring it in to him at the hospital tomorrow."

"What do you need?"

"Just a power outlet."

Robert set up the laptop on the dining room table while Vanessa opened the wine and went to find some glasses. After Robert navigated the way through the initial setup, he plugged in an external drive he had brought with him.

"What's that for?" Vanessa asked as she handed Robert his wine.

"I'm restoring all of David's files from the backups I made. It'll take a few hours."

He took the wine glass from Vanessa. "Now we can work on teaching you some calculus."

Robert picked up the calculus study guide and they both headed over to sit on the couch. Robert was doing his absolute best to explain the subject to her, but it was becoming obvious she wasn't really listening.

"I like you," she said. "I really do, no matter what happens."

"I like you too. That's why I don't want you to drop out. I'll do whatever it takes to help you pass calculus." He leaned in to kiss her.

"I can't," Vanessa said.

"What's the matter?"

"I don't want to hurt you – I really don't. Let's face it. I'm never going to pass calculus. I don't want to lead you down a path when I know there's no chance for us."

"I don't understand. We have as good a chance as anyone. We can slow things down if you want – just let things develop as we get to know each other more."

"Look – you're a great guy – you deserve better."

Robert didn't believe her. "Is there someone else?"

She smiled at him. "No, there's no one else.

Robert came over to hold her and she melted into his chest. "I wasn't supposed to let this happen," she said. "This is my fault – it's all my fault."

Suddenly they heard a beeping sound coming from the dining room.

"What's that?" Vanessa asked.

"That's just the computer," Robert said as he stroked her hair. "The files have been restored. It can wait."

Vanessa took a deep breath. She had made a decision. "It's probably best if you just get your computer and go – before we get ourselves into any more trouble."

Robert reluctantly headed into the dining room and unplugged the backup drive from the computer. He started scrolling through the list of files to make sure all the files had been copied.

"That's strange," he said.

"What is?"

"There's a whole bunch of extra files here – hundreds of them. I have no idea what they're for." He continued to scroll through the list. Then he clicked on one of them and a video started to play. "What the hell is this?"

Vanessa silently rose from the couch, pulled something from a drawer in the china cabinet and came up behind him.

"I wish you hadn't done that," she said.

"Why?"

Robert turned toward her just in time to see the butt-end of a gun hit him across the side of the head.

* * *

When Robert came to, he found his hands tied to the arms of the dining room chair. Vanessa was sitting in a chair opposite him, waiting for him to wake up. Her eyes were red and tears were streaming down her face. It was obvious she had been crying for a while.

"What's going on?" Robert asked.

"I'm sorry. You don't deserve this. I wish you and your brother had just stayed out of this whole thing."

"David? What has David got to do with this?"

"It's those files he downloaded – the ones he gave to the professor."

Robert couldn't believe what he was hearing. "Are you the one who shot David?"

Vanessa shook her head. "No, that was my partner. He's the one who shot your brother and the professor. But I was there. The agency always has a second shooter – for every mission – the backup – in case something goes wrong. I knew your brother was still alive when I was there. I was supposed to kill him, but I knew he hadn't seen what was in those files. He didn't deserve it, so I just gathered up the CDs and the gun. That should have been the end of it. Our mission was over." Vanessa came over and gently stroked the side of Robert's head where she'd hit him. "Why did you have to make a copy of the files?"

David noticed the handgun sitting on the dining room table. "You don't have to kill me. I didn't see what was in the files. Just let me go and I won't say a word – I swear."

Vanessa continued to gently stroke his head. "If I don't do it, the agency will just send someone else. I was supposed to get close to your brother to find out whether he had a copy of those files. But not too close – that would have been too obvious – so I chose you – his brother. They train us how to get close, but I crossed the line."

Vanessa picked up the gun. "You should have seen this coming. I tried to warn you, you know – while playing your stupid *Magic* game. I always chose the blue and black cards

– trickery, deception – winning at all costs. How did you not see this coming?"

"Because I fell for you. It's easy to be deceived by those you love."

"See, I knew you were too good for me. You don't deserve this. I'm sorry. I'm so, so sorry."

Vanessa raised the gun and pointed it at Robert. He closed his eyes.

Suddenly a shot rang out and blood splattered across the dining room wall. But it wasn't Robert's blood – it was Vanessa's.

Robert opened his eyes to see a man dressed all in black holding a gun. The man slowly advanced into the dining room. He pushed Vanessa's body over with his foot to make sure she was dead. Then he lowered his gun.

"You okay?" the man asked Robert.

"Yeah, I think so."

The man proceeded to untie Robert's hands from the chair. Then he started gathering up the computer and the backup drive and shoved them into the bag that Robert had brought. "Do you have any other copies of these files?"

"No."

"Good. Cause if you do, they'll keep coming for you."

"I don't. I swear. Where are you taking them?"

"I'm going to destroy them. People who come in contact with them tend to end up dead." The man picked up the bag and headed for the door.

"What should I do?"

"I'd suggest you call 9-1-1."

"Who are you? Are you the police? They'll want to know who shot Vanessa."

The man grinned. "Just tell them it was the Black Knight."

Then he was gone.

*** CHAPTER 28 ***

"We're moving you to a new room," the nurse said to David when she arrived pushing a wheelchair.

"Why? I thought you said I was going to be released tomorrow."

The nurse helped David out of bed and into the wheelchair. "As far as I know, you still are. We're moving you to the same room as your brother."

"Robert? What happened to him?"

The nurse started pushing the wheelchair down the hall. "He's fine. Got a knock on the head – probably has a concussion. He's been admitted for the night so we can keep an eye on him. He can tell you all of the details himself."

When they arrived at the new room, David saw Robert sitting up in bed. He had a big bruise on the right side of his head and it looked quite swollen. Henry was there, along with Detective Tremblay.

"What happened to you?" David asked.

"We were just about to go through the whole thing again," Detective Tremblay said.

Henry came over to help David out of the wheelchair and into the bed beside Robert's. "He almost got killed – because of those files. I told you to quit that damn secret society."

"Dad, it's not his fault," Robert said.

"Everyone should just stay calm," the detective said. He made direct eye contact with Henry to emphasize his point. "Robert, why don't you start at the beginning and take us through what happened."

Robert sighed. He had already been through it several times. "Vanessa told me earlier today that she was thinking of dropping calculus because she couldn't keep up, so I went over to her place about seven to help her study. I didn't want her to drop out. We've grown quite close over the last few weeks."

"Is that why you took a bottle of wine with you?"

"Yes – and some chocolates, but I really did want to help her with calculus too. I brought a new study guide that I got at the university bookstore."

"Why did you bring the laptop?"

Robert looked at his brother. "That was for David. I got him a new laptop to replace the computer that got stolen from the residence. Same kind as the one I got for myself a few days ago. I promised him I'd bring it to him in the hospital."

"Go on," the detective said.

"I set up the laptop on Vanessa's dining room table and then started to restore David's files from one of my backups. I knew it would take a few hours so I figured I could just let it run while Vanessa and I studied."

"Did you know what was in the files?"

"I figured it was just stuff from David's school projects. Anyway, Vanessa and I started going through the study guide – drinking wine – then I tried to make a move on her." Robert felt embarrassed saying this in front of his dad. "Then, suddenly she wanted to stop."

"Did she say why?" the detective asked.

"She said I was too good for her – said she wasn't supposed to let this happen. I figured she must already have a boyfriend or something, but she said she didn't. She asked me to leave."

"And then what happened?"

"We heard the computer beep to indicate the restoration of David's files was complete, so I went over to the dining room table to start packing everything up. I was just scrolling through the files to make sure everything was okay, but there were a bunch of extra files there. I clicked on one of them just to see what it was – a video started playing."

"Did you see what was in the video?" the detective asked.

"No. It had just started when Vanessa hit me on the side of the head and knocked me out."

"Did she say anything before she hit you?"

Robert tried to remember. "She said *I wish you hadn't done that*. When I came to, my hands were tied to the chair. There was a gun on the table. She was crying – said she had to kill me. If she didn't, they'd send someone else to do it."

"Did she say who *they* were?"

"No, I don't think so." Robert thought some more. "The *agency* – she said *the agency always sends a second shooter*."

Suddenly Robert started to remember more from that night – things that he'd forgotten until now. He looked at David. "She said it was her partner that shot David and the professor. She was the second shooter – she was supposed to kill David that night – but she let him live because he hadn't seen what was in the files."

Detective Tremblay pulled a picture from his pocket and

showed it to Robert. It was the picture of the lady with the dog. "Do you recognize her from this picture?"

Robert squinted his eyes, but it was hard for him to be sure. "I'm not sure if that's her or not – that lady's blond. But that's Wiley – that's Vanessa's dog."

Then the detective showed Robert an enhanced picture of the lady with the dog. Despite the pixilation, Robert recognized her. "That's Vanessa. She's wearing a wig – but that's her." He hung his head.

"That's not her real name," the detective said. "We still haven't figured out who she is, but the name she gave you – and the university – is fake."

"She played me," Robert said as tears streamed down his cheeks. "She said I should have seen it coming. She's right."

"Maybe we should take a break," Henry said. He could feel the pain his son was going through.

"No, I'm fine." Robert wiped his eyes and looked at the detective. "What else do you want to know?"

"Who shot Vanessa?" the detective asked.

"I don't know. Just when I thought Vanessa was going to shoot me, some guy shot her."

"Where did he come from?"

"I don't know – the kitchen maybe – I don't know how long he'd been there. After he shot Vanessa, he made sure she was dead and then he untied me."

"What did he look like?"

"He was dressed all in black – had a balaclava covering his face. He started packing up the computer. He took it with him."

"Did he say anything?"

"He asked me if I had any other copies of the files. I said I didn't. He said if I had, they'd keep coming for me." Panic spread across Robert's face. "I only saw a few seconds of the video – I swear – I have no idea what it was."

"That's okay," the detective said. "If he was watching from the kitchen, he already knows that. If he didn't, you'd probably be dead already."

The detective gave Robert a few seconds to calm himself. "Did he say anything else?"

"He said he was going to destroy the files. Then he told me to call 9-1-1. That's all I remember."

* * *

Robert was having a very rough night. Every time he would fall asleep, it wouldn't be long until he would start thrashing around in his bed as he relived his ordeal. The nurse had been in to check on him several times. At one point, she woke him from one of his nightmares to reassure him that he was now safe and sound in the hospital. There was a police officer sitting right outside their room to make sure no one could harm them.

In the bed beside him, David was also having trouble sleeping, partly because of Robert's thrashing and partly because of his own guilty feelings. His father was right. David's participation in the secret society had not only put his own life in danger, but had led to the death of the professor and almost got his brother killed. It was time to put an end to it.

David got out of bed, pulled his laptop from the hidden compartment in his soccer bag and put it on the overbed table. The nurse had told him this room had a working Internet connection. He had just started up the computer when Robert started having another nightmare. David jumped out of bed and raced over to comfort his brother.

"What time is it?" Robert asked after David woke him.

"Just after four in the morning. You were having a

nightmare."

When he was sure Robert was okay, David crawled back into his own bed.

"What are you doing awake?" Robert asked.

"I think it's about time I got out of this secret society – it's too dangerous – for everyone."

David entered the password, then entered the command to see if there were any new messages for him. "There's a new message."

"What does it say?"

"It says *Files have been destroyed – No further danger.*"

"That's good to hear. Who sends you these messages anyway?"

"I don't really know – everyone uses a code name. This message came from the *Black Knight.*"

Robert bolted up in bed. "That's the guy who shot Vanessa – the guy who saved my life. I just remembered it now when you said it."

"He's sent me several messages. He's the one who sent me the first message to watch for the second shooter. I thought it was a clue to help solve who actually killed Kennedy – but maybe it was a warning to me all along."

"Or maybe both," Robert said.

"What do you mean?"

"It was something Vanessa said. She said the agency always has a backup plan – for every mission. She said they always send a second shooter."

"What do you think I should do?"

"I'm not sure you should quit a group that probably just saved our lives. It sounds like they're watching our backs."

David thought of Bronx. He'd already lost one person who said she'd watch his back. Could he afford to lose another?

He closed the laptop.

*** CHAPTER 29 ***

Laura sat at the kitchen table at Henry's place and clicked the button on her computer to submit her latest story to the Tribune. She was sure it would also be distributed to other news agencies around the world. The public loved conspiracy stories about the Kennedy assassination, and this one was sure to add more fuel to the fire.

Laura had interviewed Robert and had written up the story that they'd found the *lady with the dog* – dead – but how police still hadn't determined her true identity. How could a person exist in this day and age without any record of who she actually was? It had to be a conspiracy. She had been killed by someone who called himself the *Black Knight* – someone who had made off with evidence that would explain who actually killed Kennedy – vanished without a trace. How could that not be a conspiracy?

"I have to head back to Chicago," Laura said as she gave both David and Robert a hug. They had finally been released from hospital and would be spending a few more days at home.

Laura threw her suitcase into the backseat of the rental

car. She gave Henry a kiss. "When's the next time you're going to be in Chicago?"

"I'm not sure." He wanted to stay pretty close to home for a while.

* * *

When Laura got to the airport, she followed the confusing directions to the rental car drop-off area. She was in the process of pulling her small suitcase out of the back seat when the rental clerk came up behind her. "Can I get your mileage?" he asked.

She recognized the voice immediately and turned toward him. "Todd, what are you doing here?"

"I just had to see you one more time before I go."

"Before you go where?"

He smiled. "I can't say where, but I won't be heading back to Chicago."

"They said you resigned from the FBI. Why?"

"I had to. We were told to stay out of the agency's way while they tried to recover those files. The FBI is *supposed* to uphold the law and protect people from all threats, even if those threats are coming from within our own government. We turned our backs on the President back in 1963. I wasn't going to let it happen again."

"So you're the *Black Knight?*"

He smiled and gave her a salute. "Agent Todd Knight – at your service."

"Have you still got those files?"

"No," Todd said. "They've already caused enough deaths. Like I told the kid – I destroyed them."

"Why? Don't you think the public has a right to know who killed Kennedy?"

"That's not my call. That's up to the current President to decide."

Laura paused before asking her next question. "Did you look at them?"

"No, but I have a pretty good idea what they'd show. I'm sure the truth will come out eventually – it always does."

"Robert owes his life to you – probably David, too."

"I should have done better," Todd said. "I was in position the night that David and the professor got shot. I was watching the lady with the dog. I was sure she was the primary shooter. The guy in the hoodie got two shots off before I could eliminate him. That's my fault. I was supposed to protect them."

Laura reached out to touch him. "It's not your fault. You couldn't have known."

Todd looked at the ground. "It's my job to know. I failed them."

Laura reached out and pulled up on Todd's chin so he was looking directly at her. "It's not your fault," she said again. But she could tell she hadn't convinced him. "So what happens now?"

"I'm going to disappear. I'm sure they've already figured out what I've done. They'll be coming for me."

"When will I see you again?"

"I don't know – maybe never. That's why I wanted to see you one last time today." He leaned in and kissed her – hard.

"You can't just disappear forever."

"Sure I can."

Suddenly another car came racing into the parking lot. A man jumped out of the driver's seat and yelled over to Todd. "I'm going to be late for my flight. Can you check the car in for me?"

"No problem, sir. I'll take care of it."

The man ran off toward the terminal.

"You better get going yourself, or you're going to miss your flight," Todd said to Laura.

Laura looked at her watch. "You're right." She turned and pulled her suitcase out of the back seat. When she turned around again, Todd was gone.

He was right. He *could* just disappear into thin air.

* * *

It was about three weeks later when David walked into his father's bedroom and saw him packing. Henry had been reluctant to travel until he was sure his boys were safe again. Robert had overcome his fears and headed back to university, confident he'd be able to catch up on his schoolwork. David felt he had fallen too far behind, so he had decided to miss the rest of the term and start fresh again after Christmas. He'd also been cut from both the Laurier and National soccer teams so he was finding it hard to get motivated about much of anything.

"I was wondering when you'd be heading off to Chicago again," David said.

"I'm not going to Chicago. I'm off to New York in the morning – supposed to investigate the costs of another merger. Laura's joining me in a few days. We're planning to see a few shows on Broadway." He briefly stopped his packing. "Are you going to be okay on your own?"

"Don't worry. I'll be fine." David's biggest fear of late was that he'd die of boredom. He started to walk down the hall toward the family room, but then turned and came back.

"Any chance I could go with you?"

"Sure. I don't see why not. But I'll be working, so I won't have much free time."

"That's okay," David said. "It's New York. Someone once told me there are a million things to do there." He opened a map that Henry had sitting on top of his suitcase and began searching for something.

"Dad, can you show me where the Bronx is?"

Other Books By

E.A. Briginshaw

Goliath

Henry Shaw leads a relatively quiet life trying to balance his work at a growing law firm with his family life, including supporting his teenage son who has a promising soccer career ahead of him. But all of that changes when Henry's bipolar brother, in one of his manic states, tells him that Goliath didn't really die as told in the biblical story – and that he is Goliath.

When his brother disappears along with a media magnate, the FBI and the local police believe they may have been part of a secret international network and that Goliath was his brother's code name. The solution to this puzzle may reside in his brother's laptop computer, which mysteriously disappears during a break-in at his house.

Is his brother dead or just hiding from forces trying to destroy the network? Henry tries to solve the puzzle along with an intriguing woman he encounters at an airport bar.

Goliath is available for purchase on the Amazon.com website.
Book   (ISBN 978-0-9921390-0-1)
eBook (ISBN 978-0-9921390-1-8)

The Legacy

Life is pretty good for the Baxter boys. Eric Baxter is a recent college graduate starting his career in financial planning. His younger brother Chip is a promising athlete heading off to compete at the Olympic Games in Brazil. And their father, Brian, has accumulated a tidy sum of money over his life.

As Eric prepares to start managing his father's money, he learns that his father's most important objective is to leave a legacy. But when Eric and his brother are kidnapped along with several other people while on a tour in Brazil, the legacy is in jeopardy.

Will the hostages be rescued before the final deadline is reached? Will Brian go against the recommendations of the FBI and the Brazilian police and pay the ransom? Their fate is determined in "The Legacy".

The Legacy is available for purchase on the Amazon.com website.
Book   (ISBN 978-0-9921390-2-5)
eBook (ISBN 978-0-9921390-3-2)

Made in the USA
Charleston, SC
28 February 2015